P9-CEK-012

Treasured Stories of Christmas

TREASURED STORIES OF
CHRISTMAS

A Touching Collection of Stories That Brings
Gifts from the Heart and Joy to the Soul

THE EDITORS OF
GUIDEPOSTS

INSPIRATIONAL PRESS
New York

Acknowledgments

Every attempt has been made to credit the sources of copyright material used in this book. If any such acknowledgment has been inadvertently omitted or miscredited, receipt of such information would be appreciated.

"The Gift That Lasts a Lifetime" by Pearl S. Buck. Copyright © 1955 by Pearl S. Buck. Reprinted by permission of Harold Ober Associates.

"The Miracle of Christmas" by Helen Steiner Rice. © 1968 by The Helen Steiner Rice Foundation. Used with permission of The Helen Steiner Rice Foundation, Cincinnati, OH.

"My Most Memorable Christmas" by Catherine Marshall. Copyright © by Marshall-LeSourd L.L.C. Used by permission.

"The Night the Angels Sang" from THE DAY CHRIST WAS BORN by Jim Bishop. Copyright © 1960 by Jim Bishop. Copyright renewed © 1988 by Betty Kelly Bishop. Reprinted by permission of HarperCollins Publishers, Inc.

"Three Symbols of Christmas" by Billy Graham. Reprinted by permission of Billy Graham Evangelistic Association.

Abridged from *The Guideposts Christmas Treasury.*

Copyright © 1972 by Guideposts.

All rights reserved. No part of this work may be reproduced or transmitted in any form or by any means, electronic, or mechanical, including photocopying, recording, or any information storage and retrieval system, without permission in writing from Guideposts, Rights & Permissions Department, 16 East 34th Street, New York, NY 10016.

First Inspirational Press edition published in 1997.

INSPIRATIONAL PRESS
A division of BBS Publishing Corporation
386 Park Avenue South, New York, NY 10016
Inspirational Press is a registered trademark of BBS Publishing Corporation.
Published by arrangement with Guideposts, Carmel, New York 10512.

Library of Congress Catalog Card Number: 97-73431
ISBN: 0-88486-180-5
Printed in the United States of America.

CONTENTS

Time for Christmas *by Fred Bauer* 12

I. *Christmas* – A TIME OF ANTICIPATION

Let Christmas Happen to You *by Norman Vincent Peale*.... 16

The Year We Had a "Sensible" Christmas *by Henry Appers* .. 21

Is Your Heart in Your Giving?............................ 28

One Step at a Time *by Carol Amen* 33

A Christmas Prayer *by Robert Louis Stevenson*........... 37

II. *Christmas* – A TIME FOR HEALING

The Christmas I Loaned My Son *by Mrs. N.H. Muller* 40

The Joy of Giving *by John Greenleaf Whittier* 42

When Christmas Came Again *by Dina Donohue* 43

A Lonely Cafeteria *by Florence Mauthe* 49

The C-C-Choir Boy *by Fred Bauer* 51

The Night the Angels Sang *by Jim Bishop* 54

The Boy with the Lonely Eyes *by Frank Graves* 56

III. *Christmas* – A TIME FOR PATIENCE

The Christmas Everything Went Wrong
    by Michael Suscavage 64

The Dime Store Angel *by Barbara Estelle Shepherd* 71

Tornado! *by Charlotte Hale Smith* 75

The Miracle of Christmas *by Helen Steiner Rice* 80

Yuletide Is Not Always So Merry *by Faith Baldwin* 81

The Failure That Helped Me Grow Up *by Penny DeFore*.... 86

IV. *Christmas* – A TIME FOR GIVING

The Gift That Lasts a Lifetime *by Pearl S. Buck* 94

A Gift of the Heart *by Norman Vincent Peale*............ 100

Christmas Bells *by Henry W. Longfellow*................ 106

Long Walk Part of Gift *by Gerald Horton Bath* 108

He's Straightest When He Stoops *by Thomas J. Fleming*... 109

V. *Christmas* – A TIME FOR UNDERSTANDING

Albert Schweitzer's Jungle Christmas *by Glenn Kittler* 112

Undelivered Gifts *by Wayne Montgomery*................ 118

Christmas Promise 121

The Christmas Song *by Glenn Kittler* 123

It Was That Night *by Fred Bauer* 125

Prayer for Peace *by St. Francis of Assisi* 126

VI. *Christmas* – A TIME FOR CHILDREN

Sit Next to Me, Please *by Robert H. Rockwell* 128

Trouble at the Inn *by Dina Donohue* 132

My Most Memorable Christmas *by Catherine Marshall* 135

She Kept Her Promise *by John Markas* 139

A Boy's Finest Memory *by Cecil B. DeMille* 142

Hope for the New Year *by Alfred Tennyson* 143

VII. *Christmas* – A TIME FOR LEARNING

Gold, Circumstance and Mud *by Rex Knowles* 146

A Boy's Christmas Discovery *by Charles E. Lesperance* 149

The Gift of a Child *by Mary Ann Matthews* 151

Contents

Pattern of Love *by Jack Smith*..................... 153

The Winner *by Glenn Kittler*..................... 155

This Quiet Night *by Rehobeth Billings* 157

VIII. *Christmas* – A TIME FOR SHARING

Holiday Candles *by Betty Girling* 160

The Family in the Parking Lot *by Norman Spray*......... 164

Let's Go Neighboring *by Leah Neustadt*................. 170

A Fragile Moment *by E.L. Huffine* 174

The Love That Lives *by W.D. Dorrity*................. 176

IX. *Christmas* – A TIME FOR LOVE

Three Symbols of Christmas *by Billy Graham* 178

What the Star Tells Us *by Fulton J. Sheen*.............. 180

The Gift of Double Joy *by Linda Leighton* 182

X. *Christmas* – A TIME FOR REMEMBERING

The Man Who Missed Christmas *by J. Edgar Parks* 186

The Miraculous Staircase *by Arthur Gordon* 192

The Runaway Boy *by Chase Walker* 200

A New Year's Prayer *by W.R. Hunt* 203

The Greatest Story Ever Told *by Saint Luke* 204

Treasured Stories of Christmas

Time for Christmas

Christmas is a time of anticipation,
When hope becomes a shining star,
When children's wishes become prayers,
And days are X'ed on calendar.

Christmas is a time for healing,
When disagreers and disagreements meet,
When long-time wounds are mended
And love moves hatred to retreat.

Christmas is a time for patience,
When we try anew to mold
Our lives in the image of Him
Whose birthday we uphold.

Christmas is a time for giving,
The Wise Men brought their best,
But Christ showed that the gift of self
Will out-give all the rest.

Christmas is a time for understanding
People and customs throughout the world,
When for all-too-brief a season,
The banner of peace is unfurled.

Christmas is a time for children
No matter what their age,
Spirit is the only ticket,
And heart the only gauge.

Christmas is a time for learning,
A time when new truths unfold,
And not-so-innocent children
Often teach the old.

Christmas is a time for sharing,
A time for needy hands to clasp,
A time for stretching out in faith
With a reach that exceeds our grasp.

Christmas is a time for love,
A time for inhibitions to shed,
A time for showing that we care,
A time for words too long unsaid.

Christmas is a time to remember
Timeless stories from days of yore,
A time to ponder what's ahead,
A time to open another door.

Fred Bauer

I

CHRISTMAS
A Time of Anticipation

Christmas is a time of anticipation,

When hope becomes a shining star,

When children's wishes become prayers,

And days are X'ed on calendar.

Let Christmas Happen to You

Norman Vincent Peale

CHRISTMAS is a season of joy and laughter when our cup of happiness brims over. Yet increasingly we hear negative remarks about what a burden the holiday season has become.

This indicates that something is wrong somewhere because Christ never meant His birthday to be anything but a glorious event. Christianity is designed for the transmission of power from Jesus Christ to the individual; a Christ-centered Christmas, therefore, should be the year's climactic experience.

Perhaps we need to use more imagination in recapturing this experience in a personal way, like some creative people are doing.

For example, in front of a Texas gasoline station there hung a big sign last December which read: "Merry Christmas and a Happy New Year to all my customers. The $150 that would be spent on your Christmas cards has gone to help the Rev. Bill Harrod bring Christmas cheer to West Dallas."

In another section of the country a church congregation was asked to bring in all the old clothes they could spare for distribution to the needy. One family sent in all new clothes, bought with money diligently saved all year to buy each other Christmas presents.

Such giving surely expressed the true meaning of the birthday of Our Lord. We best honor Him when we live the examples He set. An act of mercy that reflects the inspiration He gave us will create a deeper satisfaction and happiness than giving or receiving the most expensive gift.

Ten years ago the daughter of Mr. and Mrs. Carl Hansen of San Bernardino, California, died of cancer. She was seven years old. After time had healed some of their grief the Hansens realized their little daughter had taught them so much about a child's love that they wished to perpetuate what she had given them. They decided that Mr. Hansen would dress as Santa Claus and together they would visit every bedridden child in town who could not see Santa in the stores.

In two years they were so busy each Christmas that the Elks supplied a gift for each child they visited. Mr. Hansen learned magic to entertain the children, then collected amateur entertainers and developed a show for each visit. There were so many homes and hospitals with love-hungry children that the Hansens eventually decided to make their Christmas visiting a year-round project.

The Psalmist says: "I will remember the works of the Lord: surely I will remember thy wonders of old." The early Christians celebrated Christmas by remembering the works of the Lord and the wonders of old. It was a day for gaiety, but not for excess. There is something blasphemous and pagan about using the birthday of Jesus as an excuse for exaggerated and commercialized giving and heavy drinking. How many people do we all know who make gift-giving a burden because they spend beyond their means? In their effort to keep up with the Joneses many actually go into debt. They would better express the spirit of Christmas if their gift had more understanding in it than money. Here is an example of what I mean:

In Hewlett, Long Island, the Jewish residents formed a congregation, but did not have a temple, and met in a store. The membership outgrew the store, and right before the Christmas holiday they started a building drive for a temple. One of their neighbors, a Roman Catholic named Ricky Cardace, turned over his filling station to his Jewish friends on Christmas and New Year's Day. They would operate it, and all the receipts would go into their building fund.

So giving at Christmas can take many forms not measured by dollars. Here are a few simple suggestions for such giving:

A gift you make yourself is more appreciated—something as simple as a fruit cake or a letter opener; a surprise photo of someone's house, babies or pets. A couple we know painted the porch and front door of their parents' house. To the giver it is a labor of love; to the receiver an offering of love.

The members of one family, during a financial crisis, made personally, by hand, all gifts for each other. This particular Christmas was such a joyful one that its plan has been continued ever since.

If you know of a mother who would like to go out to church or other activities, but cannot afford a baby sitter, why not give her a gift certificate for a dozen hours of babysitting for the year to come?

Send Christmas remembrances to those who would least expect it from you; the people we often encounter but do not really know: the neighbor who nods good morning daily; the people who clean your office or workroom; the officer who directs traffic at your corner. Best of all, the person you've been most annoyed with!

Making it a point to find out more about these people is an enriching experience. Get the thrill of trips to a hospital, orphanage, a jail. Also it is a wonderful Christmas adventure to help the families of such unfortunates.

Often it is left to children to show us the way to a happier Christmas observance. The ninth grade students in Scotch Plains High School, New Jersey, decided among themselves to pool all the money they had meant to spend on Christmas gifts for each other, in class and school observances, and give it to those who needed it more. With the advice and help of their local postmistress they chose the Muscular Dystrophy Fund as the object of their generosity.

In one Western public school the sixth graders were told that in many other lands the religious expression of Christmas was its most important element, and gift-giving a minor and more often a separate part of the celebration, generally held on St. Nicholas Day. Since these lively youngsters had always been under the impression that gifts were the ultimate expression of Christmas, they were understandably surprised, and asked:

"How then should we celebrate the holiday?"

Their teacher asked them all to find the answer in the Bible: One boy wrote out this answer:

"I was hungred, and ye gave me meat: I was thirsty, and ye gave me drink . . . As ye have done it unto the least of these my brethren ye have done it unto me . . ."

That was a good beginning, the teacher told them, and suggested that they find the least of their brethren in their own town. They did, and began to collect their Christmas fund in a big, empty jar.

On Christmas Day there was enough in the jar for Christmas dinners and gifts for two families. And the children themselves took their gifts to both families. On the way back one of the teachers saw a little girl tightly clutching the empty mayonnaise jar that had held the Christmas fund.

"I'm going to put it under my tree at home," the little girl explained all aglow, "to remind me of the loveliest Christmas I've ever had."

Let such a Christ-like Christmas happen to you. You'll like it better than any Christmas you ever had.

The Year We Had a "Sensible" Christmas

Henry Appers

FOR AS LONG as I could remember our family had talked about a sensible Christmas. Every year, my mother would limp home from shopping or she would sit beside the kitchen table after hours of baking, close her eyes, catch her breath and say, "This is the last time I'm going to exhaust myself with all this holiday fuss. Next year we're going to have a *sensible* Christmas."

And always my father, if he was within earshot, would agree. "It's not worth the time and expense."

While we were kids, my sister and I lived in dread that Mom and Dad would go through with their rash vows of a reduced Christmas. But if they ever *did*, we reasoned, there were several things about Christmas that we, ourselves, would like to amend. And two of these were, namely, my mother's Uncle Lloyd and his wife, Aunt Amelia.

Many a time Lizzie and I wondered why families had to have relatives, and especially why it was our fate to inherit Uncle Lloyd and Aunt Amelia. They were a sour and a formal pair who came to us every Christmas, bringing Lizzie and me handkerchiefs as gifts and expecting in return silence, respect, service and for me to surrender my bedroom.

Lizzie and I had understood early that Great-uncle Lloyd was, indeed, a poor man, and we were sympathetic to this. But we dared to think that even poverty provided no permit for them to be stiff and unwarm and a nuisance in the bargain. Still we accepted Great-uncle Lloyd and Great-aunt Amelia as our lot and they were, for years, as much the tradition of Christmas as mistletoe.

Then came my first year in college. It must have been some perverse reaction to my being away, but Mom started it. *This* was to be the year of the sensible Christmas. "By not exhausting ourselves with all the folderol," she wrote me, "we'll at last have the energy and the time to appreciate Christmas."

Dad, as usual, went along with Mom, but added his own touch. We were not to spend more than a dollar for each of our gifts to one another. "For once," Dad said, "we'll worry about the thought behind the gift, and not about its price."

It was I who suggested that our sensible Christmas be limited to the immediate family, just the four of us. The motion was carried. Mom wrote a gracious letter to Great-uncle Lloyd explaining that what with my being away in school and for one reason and another we weren't going to do much about Christmas, so maybe they would enjoy it more if they didn't make their usual great effort to come. Dad enclosed a check, an unexpected boon.

I arrived home from college that Christmas wondering what to expect. A wreath on the front door provided a fitting nod to the season. There was a Christmas tree in the living room and I must admit that, at first, it made my heart twinge. Artificial, the tree was small and seemed without character when compared to the luxurious, forest-smelling firs of former years. But the more I looked at it, with our brightly wrapped dollar gifts under it, the friendlier it became and I began to think of the mess of real trees, and their fire threat, and how ridiculous, how really unnatural it was to bring a living tree inside a house anyway. Already the idea of a sensible Christmas was getting to me.

Christmas Eve Mom cooked a good but simple dinner and afterward we all sat together in the living room. "This is nice," Lizzie purred, a-snuggle in the big cabbage rose chair.

"Yes," Dad agreed. "It's quiet. I'm not tired out. For once, I think I can stay awake until church."

"If this were last Christmas," I reminded Mom, "you'd still be in the kitchen with your hours of 'last-minute' jobs. More cookies. More fruit cake." I recalled the compulsive way I used to nibble at Mom's fruit cake. "But I never really liked it," I confessed with a laugh.

"I didn't know that," Mom said. She was thoughtful for a moment. Then her face brightened. "But Aunt Amelia—how *she* adored it!"

"Maybe she was just being nice," Lizzie said undiplomatically.

Then we fell silent. Gradually we took to reading. Dad did slip off into a short snooze before church.

Christmas morning we slept late, and once up we breakfasted before advancing to our gifts. And what a time we had with those! We laughed merrily at our own originality and cleverness. I gave Mom a cluster-pin that I had fashioned out of aluminum measuring spoons and had adorned with rhinestones. Mother wore the pin all day or, at least, until we went out to Dempsey's.

At Dempsey's, the best restaurant in town, we had a wonderful, unrushed feast. There was only one awkward moment just after the consomme was served. We started to lift our spoons. Then Dad suggested that we say grace and we all started to hold hands around the table as we always do at home, and then we hesitated and drew our hands back, and then in unison we refused to be intimidated by a public eating place and held hands and said grace.

Nothing much happened the rest of the day. In the evening I

wandered into the kitchen, opened the refrigerator, poked around for a minute, closed the door and came back to the living room.

"That's a joke," I reported, with no idea at all of the effect my next remark would have. "I went out to pick at the turkey."

In tones that had no color, Mother spoke. "I knew that's what you went out there for. I've been waiting for it to happen."

No longer could she stay the sobs that now burst forth from her. "Kate!" Dad cried, rushing to her.

"Forgive me. Forgive me," Mom kept muttering.

"For what, dear? Please tell us."

"For this terrible, dreadful, sensible Christmas."

Each of us knew what she meant. Our Christmas had been as artificial as that Christmas tree; at some point the spirit of the day had just quietly crept away from us. In our efforts at common sense we had lost the reason for Christmas and had forgotten about others; this denied Him whose birthday it was all about. Each of us, we knew full well, had contributed to this selfishness, but Mom was taking the blame.

As her sobs became sniffles and our assurances began to take effect, Mom addressed us more coherently, in Mom's own special incoherent way. "I should have been in the kitchen last night instead of wasting my time," she began, covering up her sentimentality with anger. "So you don't like my fruit cake, Harry? Too bad. Aunt Amelia *really* adores it! And Elizabeth, even if she doesn't, you shouldn't be disrespectful to the old soul. Do you know who else loves my fruit cake? Mrs. Donegan down the street loves it. And she didn't get her gift from me this year. Why? Because we're being *sensible*." Then Mom turned on Dad, wagging her finger at him. "We can't afford to save on Christmas, Lewis! It shuts off the heart."

That seemed to sum it up.

Yet, Lizzie had another way of saying it. She put it in a letter to me at school, a letter as lovely as Lizzie herself. "Mom feels," Lizzie wrote, "that the strains and stresses are the birth pangs of Christmas. So do I. I'm certain that it is out of our efforts and tiredness and turmoil that some sudden, quiet, shining, priceless thing occurs each year and if all we produce is only a feeling as long as a flicker, it is worth the bother."

Just as my family came to call that The Christmas That Never Was, the next one became the Prodigal Christmas. It was the most festive, and the most frazzling time in our family's history—not because we spent any more money, but because we threw all of ourselves into the joy of Christmas. In the woods at the edge of town we cut the largest tree we'd ever had. Lizzie and I swathed the house in greens. Delicious smells came from the kitchen as Mom baked and baked and baked. . . . We laughed and sang carols and joked.

Even that dour pair, Great-uncle Lloyd and Great-aunt Amelia, were almost but not quite gay. Still, it was through them that I felt that quick surge of warmth, that glorious "feeling as long as a flicker," that made Christmas meaningful.

We had just sat down in our own dining room and had reached out our hands to one another for our circle of grace. When I took Great-aunt Amelia's hand in mine, it happened. I learned something about her and giving that, without this Christmas, I might never have known.

The hand that I held was cold. I became aware of how gnarled her fingers were, how years of agonizing arthritis had twisted them. Only then did I think of the handkerchiefs that Lizzie and I had received this year, as in all the years before. For the first time I saw clearly the delicate embroidery, the painstaking needlework—Great-aunt Amelia's yearly gift of love to, and for, us.

Is Your Heart in Your Giving?

How To Give

THE BIBLE ABOUNDS with advice on *how* to give. Paul tells us that we should give *not grudgingly, or of necessity: for God loveth a cheerful giver.* And in Matthew we are warned *to take heed that ye do not your alms before men, to be seen of them. . . .*

These practical suggestions, and more, are echoed and restated by a remarkable man of the Middle Ages who put forth what he called "The Golden Ladder of Charity." Moses ben Maimon, who is known to us as Maimonides (1135-1204), was a Jewish philosopher-physician-astronomer-rabbi who greatly influenced the thinking and doctrine of not only his own religion but of Christian and Islamic thinking as well. In each of the steps of his Golden Ladder there is something for us to recognize—and to ponder.

Read through carefully the following eight steps; then, in the space designated, write in one or more personal gifts you have made in the past year that correspond to Maimonides' definition.

"THE FIRST and lowest degree is to give—but with reluctance or regret. This is the gift of the *hand* but not of the *heart*.

"THE SECOND is to give cheerfully, but not proportionately to the distress of the suffering.

"THE THIRD is to give cheerfully, and proportionately, but not until we are solicited.

"THE FOURTH is to give cheerfully, proportionately, and even unsolicited; but to put it in the poor man's hand, thereby exciting in him the painful emotion of shame.

"THE FIFTH is to give charity in such a way that the distressed may receive the bounty and know their benefactor, without their being known to him. Such was the conduct of our ancestors, who used to tie up money in the hind-corners of their cloaks, so that the poor might take it unperceived.

"THE SIXTH, which rises still higher, is to know the objects of our bounty, but remain unknown to them. Such was the conduct of those of our ancestors who used to convey their charitable gifts into people's dwellings, taking care that their own persons should remain unknown.

"THE SEVENTH Is still more meritorious; namely, to bestow charity in such a way that the benefactor may not know the relieved persons, nor they the name of their benefactor.

"THE EIGHTH and most meritorious of all is to anticipate charity by preventing poverty; namely, to assist the reduced brother either by a considerable gift, or a loan of money, or by teaching him a trade, or by putting him in the way of business, so that he may earn an honest livelihood and not be forced to the dreadful alternative of holding up his hand for charity. This is the highest step and the summit of charity's Golden Ladder."

How many of the eight kinds of giving were you able to recount in your own experience? Did you find your list thinning out near the end? Most of us at Guideposts did.

An Experiment

If you found your giving superficial, lacking the depth of true gifts from the heart, perhaps you would like to try an experiment this Christmas season. Here is the way it works:

In addition to your regular Christmas giving plan, or in place of it, make out a special list solely of gifts of self. It could include things you make, cook or grow; also visits to the lonely, gifts of time for babysitting, letters of appreciation. One of the best gifts of all could be the simple asking of forgiveness of someone you have wronged.

In preparing a Christmas card list, include people who would least expect but most appreciate a remembrance from you. Go back through the years—what people have you lost track of? Include them too. Then send one to the person you most dislike. Use your imagination in creating a list that you think would most please God.

Keep Trying

After Christmas go back to the Golden Ladder of Charity and see if you can fill in the rungs near the top, especially six, seven and eight. Make note of your successes and failures and vow to improve your approach to giving in the months that lay ahead. Ask God to help you be more sensitive to the needs of others and less concerned about the cost to self.

In conclusion, remember that gracious giving requires no special talent, nor large sums of money. It is compounded of the heart and head acting together toward the perfect expression of the spirit. It is love sharpened with imagination. The best gift is always a portion of oneself.

One Step at a Time

Carol Amen

I SAT AT THE sewing machine staring at that pile of work.

The cut-out pieces of three bathrobes, a jumper and a blouse waited for me to transform them into gifts. I would never get them done by Christmas with everything else I had to do. Christmas was only eight days off now—only four of them school days in which to work secretly on these surprise projects.

I stared out the window which supplied a scant, gray winter's light to my sewing area, then back at the pile of work, trying to decide which garment to start on.

Actually, I felt like chucking the whole thing. I had wanted to sew in order to give my family exactly what they needed without spending too much money.

It seemed ironic to be making things for those I loved and hating every minute of it. What was the matter with me? I had been sitting there 15 minutes without sewing a single stitch.

I looked away from the sewing machine and peered out into the cold deserted street. Not even the usual hardy preschoolers were anywhere to be seen. And then, to my left, like a slow human snail, appeared Mr. Andrews bundled under coat, muffler and hat, and preceded by his cane.

Mr. Andrews was as new to the neighborhood as the rest of us—residents of about three months. He had told my son (size 14 bathrobe) that a stroke two years ago had left him helpless in bed for a long time. In recent months he had relearned to walk. "Just like a baby does," he had told my son. He had to practice every day or he'd regress. We met him often and always waved, but he could only nod slightly. It took every bit of concentration he could muster to command his legs and arms to coordinate his slow trek to the end of the street and back.

Now, curiously drawn by his jerky *tap-tap*, I watched him, letting the robe pieces fall neglected into my lap. His progress was slow. Each step carried him about six inches forward.

How far it must seem to him to his goal—the end of the street, turn and shuffle slowly home, I thought. Then I gasped as I saw an obstacle. Because it was garbage collection day, neighbors had set their cans out by the street. But at the house directly across from us, they blocked the whole sidewalk. In order to get by, Mr. Andrews would have to step off the curb or balance himself on the slight incline of the driveway.

I watched him pause and study his problem. Half rising from my chair, I decided to run downstairs and outside to help, but he had started his detour alone. I stayed at the window hypnotized. Slowing from the already short, careful steps, Mr. Andrews began a series of even smaller inchings down the slope of the driveway. Once he tottered and almost fell, but instead of wasting breath calling out, he precariously steadied himself and proceeded. One foot and then the other—not always strong and sure but always determined, he moved on past the cans. Ever so slowly he edged back up the slope and onto the flat and ever so patiently on and on down the sidewalk.

I examined the pile of unattached bathrobe parts through a hot flush of shame. If I had not been stymied into inactivity by the overwhelmingness of my task, I could have had the first set of pockets on already. It embarrassed me to draw the comparison out fully. Here I sat with all my faculties intact except one—the will to begin, to take the first step. And there was Mr. Andrews.

He seemed to be speaking to me across the distance which separated us. *You can't get anywhere if you don't start,* floated one message on the gray winter day, and another was, *You can only go anywhere one step at a time.* I realized that my sewing machine, the same as Mr. Andrews' faltering legs, contained no magic. Work was required.

By the time his cane *tap-tapped* back in the other direction, I had the fronts and back attached with neat seams. I worked steadily the rest of that day and had size 14 finished and hidden away just as the school bus arrived.

I enjoyed the days that remained before Christmas. With a stack of carols on the record player, I hummed while stitching, and completed one gift each day. At exactly three o'clock on the Friday school was out, I wrapped the last outfit, my daughter's jumper and blouse, and placed it under the tree. If I had wasted five more minutes anywhere along the line, I'd never have finished in time.

A Christmas Prayer

LOVING FATHER, help us remember the birth of Jesus, that we may share in the song of the angels, the gladness of the shepherds, and the worship of the wise men.

Close the door of hate and open the door of love all over the world.

Let kindness come with every gift and good desires with every greeting.

Deliver us from evil by the blessing which Christ brings, and teach us to be merry with clear hearts.

May the Christmas morning make us happy to be Thy children, and the Christmas evening bring us to our beds with grateful thoughts, forgiving and forgiven, for Jesus' sake. Amen!

Robert Louis Stevenson

II

CHRISTMAS

A Time for Healing

Christmas is a time for healing,

When disagreers and disagreements meet,

When long-time wounds are mended

And love moves hatred to retreat.

The Christmas I Loaned My Son

Mrs. N. H. Muller

Q.: IS THERE any place where we can borrow a little boy three or four years old for the Christmas holidays? We have a nice home and would take wonderful care of him and bring him back safe and sound. We used to have a little boy, but he couldn't stay, and we miss him so when Christmas comes. – N.M.

A.: If anyone has a little boy to lend over Christmas, write to this column as early as possible, marking "Christmas" on outside of envelope.

As I read the above appeal in our local newspaper something happened to me: for the first time since my husband's death I thought of grief as belonging to someone else. I read and reread the letter to the editor. Should I answer it? Could I answer it?

When I received word from Washington that my husband had been killed in service overseas, I'd taken my little son and moved back to the tiny village of my birth.

I'd gone to work to help support my son and time had helped to erase a few scars in my heart and to soften the blow of my husband's passing. But there were special times when the ache would return and loneliness would engulf me. Birthdays, our wedding anniversary and holidays. . . .

This particular Christmas the old pain was returning when my eyes caught the appeal in the newspaper column.

We used to have a little boy, but he couldn't stay and we miss him so when Christmas comes. . . .

I, too, knew what missing was, but I had my little boy. I knew how empty the sparkle of Christmas is unless you see it by the candles of joy in a child's eyes.

I answered the appeal. The writer of the letter was a widower who lived with his mother. He had lost his beloved wife and his little son the same year.

That Christmas my son and I shared a joyous day with the widower and his mother. Together, we found a happiness that we doubted would ever be ours again.

But the best part is that this joy was mine to keep throughout the years and for each of the 10 Christmases since. You see, the man who wrote the letter became my husband.

The Joy of Giving

Somehow not only for Christmas
But all the long year through,
The joy that you give to others
Is the joy that comes back to you.

And the more you spend in blessing
The poor and lonely and sad,
The more of your heart's possessing
Returns to make you glad.

John Greenleaf Whittier

When Christmas Came Again

Dina Donohue

MANY PEOPLE knew that Frank Hinnant had no use for Christmas, but few understood the reasons why he had shut Christmas out of his heart.

As the head of his own multimillion dollar contracting business, Frank discouraged Yuletide office parties each year. He gave no Christmas bonuses. It was enough that his employees received pay increases when merited and fringe benefits more generous than any firm in town.

His wife, Adele, was of a different fabric. She loved Christmas and she longed to celebrate it fully, with all the fuss she could stir up. It was the one chronic disagreement the Hinnants had. Each December they renewed the argument. Adele wanted decorations, a tree, gifts, even parties for employees—and Frank said, emphatically, "No." Dutifully he would go along to other people's parties, he would go to Christmas services as usual, and for Adele there would always be a string of pearls or a costly, but tasteful, pin—but beyond that, "Nonsense," Frank would say, "Christmas is for children!"

And that is precisely the reason Frank Hinnant had locked
Christmas out of his heart—children.

One morning, a brisk, December day, Frank decided to walk
to work. He did this occasionally, varying his route each time. Frank
was a man with a giant curiosity, fascinated by people, where they
lived, and how. This morning, reaching mid-town, he noticed a
cluster of people standing in front of Leeson's Department Store.
They were looking at the Christmas displays, each on a different
theme.

One window had a manger scene. Frank looked at the creche:
at Mary, Joseph and the shepherd in colorful costumes; the donkey,
cow and sheep—all were life-size. And there was the Child.

Frank turned away.

He started to move on. As he did, a sign across the street caught
his fleeting attention.

"Holy Innocents Home"—huge golden letters framed the arched
doorway of an old brownstone building surrounded by a forbidding
iron fence. Frank had only half noticed this building before. Even
now it had a way of shrinking into the urban landscape.

"Holy Innocents . . . Holy Innocents. . . ." Frank repeated the
name in his mind. He stood there staring at the orphanage across
the street, and yet he was seeing something else, something far
beyond, a long ago morning in Sunday school. There was Miss Ray-

mond, a skinny woman with black hair pulled back into a knot, and Miss Raymond was telling the class about King Herod and all the male children under two, ". . . and the wicked king had had these little children slaughtered because he feared the Baby Jesus. . . ."

"The Holy Innocents," Frank said to himself. "That's odd, you don't hear about them much. Christmas is just this sentimental mush, like Adele's joy-on-earth stuff. There's more to Christmas than syrup. There's misery too."

Frank turned back to the windows of Leeson's. He looked at the smiles on the benign faces of Mary and Joseph. But what about the parents of the infants who had died? What about *their* faces?

And for the millionth time Frank remembered the desolation of the day that David had died.

David had been 18 months old. In the 22 years since then, Frank had not been able to bring himself to mention his son's name.

Frank walked on towards his office. At the corner he turned and looked back. "The Holy Innocents," he said, almost out loud.

Impulsively he struck out on a new course. An idea had come to him. Quickly he covered the four blocks to the public library, then up the steps and in, arriving at the information desk to fairly demand one reference book after another. Librarians began to heap tomes in front of him and Miss Summerwell herself stayed by his side to render assistance.

"Holy Innocents," reported Miss Summerwell, book in hand, finger pointing, "Their feast day is celebrated on December 28 by the Anglican and Roman Catholic churches, on December 29 by the Greek Orthodox church. They are among the early martyrs. . . ."

The information mounted, some of it conflicting. Some sources stated that thousands of infants had been slaughtered by Herod, others reported only a few. Frank was most impressed by the historian who very carefully deduced that since only about 2,000 people were living then in Bethlehem, no more than 20 children had been killed.

"Imagine that," he shouted to Miss Summerwell, "only 20 children!"

Very politely Miss Summerwell asked this extraordinary man to try to keep his voice a little lower.

When Frank left the public library that day he still did not go to his office. He headed back to Holy Innocents Home.

That evening, Frank and Adele dined alone. It was a leisurely dinner, yet Frank was ill at ease. He was searching for the right moment, the right phrases to use when he told Adele what, sooner or later, he had to tell her.

"I had an odd kind of day," he plunged in finally. "I went to visit an orphanage."

Adele wouldn't have been more taken aback if Frank had said he'd flown to the Hebrides for lunch, but, having lived with Frank a long time, she registered only the mildest curiosity.

"It's that bastille of an orphanage across from Leeson's," Frank ambled on. "Really a dungeon, dear, cramped and dismal. . . ."

Adele was fascinated. Frank was building up to something. Now he told about the walk downtown, about the creche at Leeson's. At last he told her about his visit to the orphanage itself. "It made me realize how little I really know about kids. What strange little ugly creatures they are! When I went in they stood around looking at me like I was a movie star, not one of them saying anything. Later one of them came up to me—I'll never forget it—this little boy came up and he stood there and he stroked the sleeve of my coat."

Adele was quiet. It was her eyes that urged him to continue. But Frank was embarrassed now. "You know full well what I've always said about Christmas," he blustered. "Christmas is for children!"

"Yes, you've always said that."

"Well, it's about time people started doing something for them. Today I gave that place some money. They're going to build a wing with it."

Adele was swept away by the kindness of this man she had loved so long. She thought she knew him completely, but she was unprepared for his next announcement. "They're going to name the wing for David."

It was the first time in 22 years that Adele had heard Frank mention their only son's name. It made her do something she never did when Frank was around. She wept.

Frank never told her about that moment. He never told her how, as he held her in his arms, he saw again something he had envisioned for the first time that afternoon. He saw a room full of children. There were 20 of them playing in a bright new wing at Holy Innocents. But now, suddenly, instead of 20, there were 21.

A Lonely Cafeteria

Florence Mauthe

ON CHRISTMAS morning the cafeteria looked sterile—white table-cloths, cold tiled floors, and white-uniformed counter girls and bus-boys bustling about. Even the Christmas tree set up in the corner did nothing to dispel my feelings of depression as I arrived to begin my duties as supervisor.

The first customers arriving for breakfast were the elderly residents of the hotel. This morning, as they did each day, they put their food on their trays, paid the cashier and then each went to a lonely separate table. One or two ventured a hesitant "Merry Christmas," but there was no warmth in their voices.

Forgetting my own resentment at having to leave a warm home to work on Christmas, I began to walk among the tables, nodding to customers and trying to smile the "Merry Christmas" I did not really feel. Then from the corner of my eye, I spotted four of the busboys in a huddle. Thinking they were dawdling, I started to reprimand them, but before I could speak out, I heard some barely audible sounds: *Our Father, Which art in Heaven, Hallowed be Thy name.*

The boys were singing, and now the melody rose and flowed through the room, quiet but beautiful in muted harmony.

Faces came alive with surprise and reverence. One of the boys turned off the lights. Only the tree glowed then, its lights reflecting the gay bulbs and tinsel. The prayer ended, and the room was hushed. Someone sighed. Then the boys sang *Silent Night, Adeste Fideles* and *Hark, the Herald Angels Sing.* As they sang, they moved about the room, working and encouraging the timid to join in the caroling.

When breakfast was over, the conversation was warm and animated and the diners moved reluctantly from the room. Someone shouted, "Merry Christmas," and his words were echoed all down the line.

Over these tired, lonely, old faces had swept the transforming spirit of Christmas—a spirit that never pales, never ages, never loses its power.

The C-C-Choir Boy

Fred Bauer

EVERYONE was surprised—everyone except Mrs. Brown, the choir director—when Herbie showed up in November to rehearse for the church's annual Christmas cantata.

Mrs. Brown wasn't surprised because she had persuaded Herbie to "at least try." That was an accomplishment, for lately he had quit trying nearly everything—reciting in class, playing ball or even asking his brothers or sisters to pass the potatoes.

It was easy to understand: He stuttered. Not just a little, either, and sometimes when his tongue spun on a word, like a car on ice, the kids laughed. Not a big ha-ha laugh, but you can tell when people are laughing at you even if you're only nine.

Mrs. Brown had figured Herbie could sing with the other tenors—Charley and Billy—and not have any trouble, which is exactly the way it worked. Billy was given the only boy's solo and the rest of the time the three of them sang in unison, until Charley contracted the measles. Even so, Billy had a strong voice and Herbie knew he could follow him.

At 7:15, the night of the cantata, a scrubbed and combed Herbie arrived at church, wearing a white shirt, a new blue and yellow bow tie and his only suit, a brown one with high-water pant legs. Mrs. Brown was waiting for him at the door.

"Billy is home in bed with the flu," she said. "You'll have to sing the solo." Herbie's thin face grew pale.

"I c-c-can't," he answered.

"We need you," Mrs. Brown insisted.

It was unfair. He wouldn't do it. She couldn't make him. All of these thoughts tumbled through Herbie's mind until Mrs. Brown told him this:

"Herbie, I know you can do this—with God's help. Across from the choir loft is a stained-glass window showing the manger scene. When you sing the solo, I want you to sing it only to the Baby Jesus. Forget that there is anyone else present. Don't even glance at the audience." She looked at her watch. It was time for the program to begin.

"Will you do it?"

Herbie studied his shoes.

"I'll t-t-try," he finally answered in a whisper.

A long 20 minutes later, it came time for Herbie's solo. Intently, he studied the stained-glass window. Mrs. Brown nodded, and he opened his mouth, but at that exact instant someone in the congregation coughed.

"H-H-Hallelujah," he stammered. Mrs. Brown stopped playing and started over. Again, Herbie fixed his eyes on the Christ Child. Again, he sang.

"Hallelujah, the Lord is born," his voice rang out, clear and confident. And the rest of his solo was just as perfect.

After the program, Herbie slipped into his coat and darted out a back door—so fast that Mrs. Brown had to run to catch him. From the top of the steps, she called, "Herbie, you were wonderful. Merry Christmas."

"Merry Christmas to you, Mrs. Brown," he shouted back. Then, turning, he raced off into the night through ankle-deep snow—without boots. But then he didn't really need them. His feet weren't touching the ground.

The Night the Angels Sang

Jim Bishop

JOSEPH APOLOGIZED to Mary. He was sorry that the Hospice of Chamaan had no room for her and ashamed that he had failed her in this hour.

Mary studied her husband, a tender smile on her face. She told her husband that he had not failed her; he had been good and tender and lawful. Mary looked around at the haltered cattle, the few lambs, some asses and a camel. If it is the will of God, she said, that His son be born in a place like this, she would not question it.

She asked Joseph to go outside and tend the fire and to remain there until she called him. Joseph did so, heating the water and praying . . . when he heard a tiny, thin wail. He wanted to rush in at once. He got to this feet, and moved no further. She would call.

"Joseph." It was a soft call, but he heard it. He hurried inside.

Mary smiled at her husband as he bent far over to look. There among the cloths, he saw the tiny red face of an infant. This, said Joseph to himself, is the one of whom the angels spoke. He dropped to his knees.

Down in the valley, sheep huddled against the chill—when the deep night sky was split with light. The sleeping shepherds awakened and, in fear, hid their eyes in the folds of their garments. Then, an angel appeared in bodily form, standing in air over the valley.

"Do not fear," the angel said slowly. "I bring you good news of great joy. A Saviour, who is the Lord Messias, was born to you today in David's town. And this shall serve you as a token: You will find an infant wrapped in swaddling clothes and cradled in a manger."

There was nothing frightening in that news. It had been promised by God a long time ago. The shepherds knew that they were not sleeping. This thing was happening; happening to lonely and despised men in a valley beneath Bethlehem.

They were still dwelling on the wonders of God and His works when the angel was joined by hundreds of others, who appeared brightly in the night sky, and began to sing in a heavenly chorus:

"Glory to God in the heaven above, and on earth peace to men of good will."

The Boy with the Lonely Eyes

Frank Graves[1]

THE FIRST TIME I met Jim Patterson, I had the feeling that he was going to spit at me. Contempt, that was the impression this 15-year-old boy gave. He looked with suspicion at the hand I offered; if the judge hadn't been there I doubt he would have bothered to shake it.

But there was something else about him: his eyes. They were so sad, so passive, so melancholy. Without question, he had the loneliest eyes I have ever seen.

So this was the boy the court wanted me to take back to Boys Republic! Obviously Jim Patterson didn't want to come. And to tell the truth, at first I didn't want him there. I'd had plenty of experience with his quiet, surly type. It's always easier, I said to myself, with the steam-spouters.

Certainly we didn't have to accept him. Our farm-school community is a private undertaking, held together by the generosity of friends and held up, often, by its own bootstraps. It's non-profit and non-sectarian and though most of its 125 14- to 18-year-olds are

[1] Director of Boys Republic, Chino, California

indeed wards of the California juvenile courts, we only accept those troubled boys who we think will benefit from our type of life. Self-government, self-discipline, work, sunshine—these are the things that Boys Republic, since 1907, has represented.

Later, alone with me, the judge said, "Take him out there with you, Mr. Graves. It's hard to get him to talk, I know, but he's bright and I have a strong, experienced hunch that he's eager to work. He's hungry to be himself."

The boy's record showed a bizarre upbringing. Both his mother and father were alcoholics; he was their only child. Sometimes they had beaten him, but what was worse, they neglected him. They'd lock him in his room without food for days on end. When he stole money from a cash register one day, his peculiar family background was revealed, and the court placed him in a foster home.

All had gone well for awhile. Jim seemed to warm to normal home life; apparently he liked his foster parents. And then he was caught in a department store stealing an electric hair dryer; he said that he had wanted to give it to his foster mother for her birthday. His fate now lay at the discretion of the court and the court wanted him to go to Boys Republic.

While driving the 40 miles from Los Angeles to Chino that January afternoon, I soon gave up trying to draw Jim Patterson into conversation. He sat there staring out of the window as though he were being kidnapped. He wasn't a handsome lad. He didn't even have the "cuteness" of youth. He wasn't tough-looking nor was he sweet-looking. He was just a boy—thin, pallid, angry.

The hill upon which our 215-acre farm is built was green from the winter rains. Jim received without comment my little travelogue. "There's the football field. That's the laundry and over there's the dairy. The boys do all the work, you know. It's a self-help system."

I took him to one of the five cottages where the boys live and introduced him to his "Granny"—his housemother—and then he slipped into the stream of routine living.

During the next weeks I waited for reports on him, but nothing of any significance was ever registered. If I asked his chaplain or counselor how Jim was faring, the reply would be a non-committal one.

"Patterson? Very quiet boy. No. Nothing in particular to report."

It was strange how Jim Patterson gnawed at me. I thought I knew boys, but this one—was he a time bomb who had to explode one day?

The Republic's most important industry—for one frantic month it absorbs us almost totally—is the making of Christmas wreaths. It started as a hobby with our founder, Margaret Fowler, and then, during a period of great financial need, the boys began to make them in quantity for sale. Today it is a giant enterprise that saves us from having to make mail appeals for money.

Throughout the year the boys go out on field trips to gather leaves and cones and pods for these wreaths. When all the different ingredients have been gathered in, they are dried, drilled, wired, and finally stored in great bins until the last week in November. Then the redwood greenery comes down from the North and the Republic turns into a massive assembly line.

Each boy is given a free wreath to send out to whomever he chooses each year, and I noticed, as the wreath-making began, that Jim addressed his to the foster parents who had been so kind to him.

Then, at last, a counselor told me something unusual about Jim. "He says he wants to make some money."

Suddenly, I was concerned. What did Jim have in mind? The boys are given a very small allowance but when they want to make extra money they have to work extra hours. It's not easy, especially around wreath-time. I became fascinated by Jim's industry. He'd be up early at the dairy. At mealtimes he'd be in the kitchen washing dishes. Until late at night he'd load boxes at the government post-office set up for our Christmas rush.

I didn't learn what he was going to do with his extra money until the day before Christmas: I was talking to his housemother when Jim walked by. He was as silent and as unresponsive as ever.

"By the way," Mrs. Garnes whispered to me, "the mystery is solved. Jim used that money he worked for to buy a wreath."

"Another wreath!" I said, surprised and bewildered.

"Yes," she went on, "he sent it to his parents—his real parents, that is."

Time bomb? I had spent a year waiting for that boy to explode. There, talking to Mrs. Garnes, I almost wept. Jim Patterson had exploded all right, but in his own way, gently, with an act of goodness.

In the time he had been with us, this silent, deceptive-looking boy had learned everything we had tried to teach him about honesty and diligence and effort. But most of all he had mastered what perhaps is hardest for all men: to love people who do not love us.

Periodically we have a kind of graduation ceremony during which our boys receive their Republic citizenship certificates. The time came for Jim to "terminate," and I was heading out of my office on the way to the ceremonies when, to my amazement, I found him waiting for me in the hall. "Mr. Graves," he said.

"Yes, Jim."

"May I walk down the hall with you?"

"Sure," I nodded, and he fell into stride with me. Together we headed toward the assembly hall. I waited for him to say something, but he didn't. We walked the entire distance in silence. Then, we came to the door and both of us stopped. He turned and looked up at me.

His eyes still had that far away, lonely look, the same as the first time I saw him. But there was a difference. Now he was really trying to reach out to me.

"Well," he said, "so long, Mr. Graves." Then he stood back to let me enter.

In a way it was the most beautiful conversation I ever had.

III

CHRISTMAS

A Time for Patience

Christmas is a time for patience,

When we try anew to mold

Our lives in the image of Him

Whose birthday we uphold.

The Christmas Everything Went Wrong

Michael Suscavage

ON DECEMBER 25, 1968, we had been married exactly 26 days. Linda and I had looked forward to our first Christmas in that special, exciting way that turned everything we did together into an historic first. It was as though we were consciously creating and storing up memories, and we wanted this Christmas to be as perfect as possible.

It was Linda's idea that we invite my parents to come into New York from New Jersey for Christmas dinner at our apartment. They needed a change of scene, she reasoned, since I, of course, was so recently married and my brother Wayne would not be able to be home for the holidays; Wayne was in Vietnam. We insisted they come in spite of the difficulties we knew we faced.

There was our apartment, for instance. *Some* apartment! A not-large living room, a not-large bedroom, a microscopic kitchen, a sprinkling of handsome wedding gifts and a few peculiarities of furniture.

For this honeymoon palace we paid a sum of money that would keep us constantly broke, but it was located on the convenient and nice East Side of Manhattan, exactly where we wanted to live. We felt it worth our scrimping.

"Your mother and dad understand our apartment," Linda said. "I'll work my wiles on a turkey. We have plenty of china and silver, and I'll go out and find the best-looking Christmas tree in town. We'll have this place looking more Christmasy than the North Pole. It will be a Christmas to remember."

Her enthusiasm had convinced me.

But we had not counted on Linda's getting an assignment. She's an airline stewardess, and though she was not originally scheduled to fly Christmas Eve, there was a sudden call for her that morning that sent her scurrying out of the house for a flight to Denver. And neither of us counted on Dan Sawyer, my roommate from bachelor days, who, on the afternoon of Christmas Eve, told me he couldn't make it back to his folks in Syracuse. What else could I do but ask him to come spend Christmas with us?

So it was that Dan came home with me from my office Christmas Eve. "Meet the Christmas tree my dear wife paid twenty dollars for," I said to him as we forced our way into the apartment. All eight feet of the homely pine lay lifeless in the narrow hallway as if it had been hacked to the ground on that very spot. I was not disposed to liking that tree. Its needles now littered the room, and already it had managed to insinuate itself as an argument between Linda and me. Linda, I felt, had gone hog-wild on that monstrosity—a "bargain" for such a "beauty" at New York prices, or so she had told me. Even so, she knew full well how carefully we were supposed to be watching every penny. I was genuinely angry at her extravagance.

"We can't just leave it there," Danny said hours later as we sat staring at the tree. Ever since we arrived home it had been a stumbling block as we went back and forth to the refrigerator, rummaging for food and drink. "I think we'd better set it up."

"With what?" I asked. "We have no stand, no decorations and, thanks to Linda, no extra money."

Danny insisted we do something. Finally we succeeded in propping up the tree with our brand-new encyclopedia and, for security, nudging the monster against the wall. It was a pathetic sight.

That superhuman task completed, we relaxed. We talked. We mused about past Christmases, about all the preparations that used to keep our homes abuzz. Danny remembered, too, how efficient my mother had always been—the gifts carefully wrapped and set aside, the tree meticulously decorated, the meals fabulously planned.

Danny and I sat there in that drab room. From the couch I could look into the bedroom and see the pictureless walls and the sheets Linda and I had hung over the windows in lieu of curtains. And when

I looked over at that bare Christmas tree, I felt just a little forlorn myself.

It must have been after midnight when the door buzzer shattered the melancholy. In no time the red and green of a very familiar airline uniform appeared in the room. Linda was home earlier than expected! But she was tired. Her eyes seemed to reflect overwork, and her long blond hair fell colorlessly to her weary shoulders. She gave me a tiny kiss and, if disappointed at seeing poor old Danny there, she didn't really show it. Then the tree caught her eye.

"The tree! The tree! You put it up!" She stood back to appraise it. "Ah, such *character*," she said in total approval, as a kind of twinkle returned to her. "You see, it *was* twenty dollars well spent. It transforms the room." Danny and I just looked at each other.

"Did you find the cranberries and popcorn?" she asked, turning to the kitchen. It was the first I had heard about them. "Good—you waited for me. We'll fix them and string them for the tree and cut out paper stars."

Linda darted into the kitchen and for the next several hours rattled and clanged and mumbled as she struggled to thaw and then stuff a half-frozen turkey. I proved inept at stringing cranberries, partly because the sewing needle Linda suggested I use was too small for the string she suggested I use. We never learned how to pop the corn properly. And the master of the paper-star department, Danny, wielded his scissors clumsily. In fact, more than anything, Danny was in the way. Annoyed, I said to him, "Just forget the stars." A smile could not hide his disappointment nor mask the flush in his face.

At 3:30 a.m. we called it quits. We all knew what a fiasco it had been. I blamed myself for having been angry about the cost of the tree, and for having been so helpless. And now I felt additionally helpless; I didn't know what I could do for Linda, who had tried so hard with so little to show for it. She made up the couch for our guest. The only good moment of the whole Christmas Eve came as I was closing our bedroom door and saw Danny in the living room, squatting before the Christmas tree, placing two little packages beneath its bare branches.

Too early in the morning Linda was up putting the turkey in the oven. Somehow the three of us stumbled off to an early church service and when we came back, we were so tired that we all went back to bed. Linda set the alarm, but it didn't go off. The extra rest was good for us, but not for the bird in the oven. Linda was distraught. Christmas dinner, she said, was "ruined." I didn't know what to say; I didn't know how to comfort her.

And at just that terrible moment, my family arrived: Mother and Dad, their arms filled with packages, and to my surprise, Virginia, my brother Wayne's wife, was with them, her arms filled too. Not all of those packages were Christmas gifts. As though psychic, Mother had brought jars of her summer canning, some special pastries, a Christmas letter to us from Wayne, a large supply of her famous salad and dozens of the family Christmas-tree ornaments I recognized immediately. "I made a mince pie too, dear," Mother said to Linda, "but I burned it to a crisp."

Hearing about the mince pie had a strange and happy effect on Linda. "Have you ever had charcoal turkey?" Linda asked Mom, all twinkling again as the two of them disappeared, if I may use the expression, into the kitchen.

The turkey was dry all right, but surprisingly tasty. We marveled at it, and joked. And that was the tenor of the day. That was the way the day eased on. We sat at our makeshift dining table with our beautiful wedding china and crystal, and we enjoyed just being there together. At one special point, we remembered Wayne. My father led us in a prayer for his safe return and for peace everywhere. It was an appropriate ending for a lovely and loving day.

After everyone had gone, Linda and I sat together in what was now a very cluttered room, before a very beautiful tree. Linda said, "I think I understand when Christmas is most perfect—when *things* are most imperfect. Then people begin to depend on each other."

Linda was right. The more important we make things, the less important people become. We can work for, and hope for, a "perfect" Christmas, but the more we are caught up in engineering it, the more readily its mystery eludes us. Christmas is Christ's day, not our day, but He has a way of sharing it with us as we share with one another.

The Dime Store Angel

Barbara Estelle Shepherd

WHEN OUR TWIN daughters were toddlers and Scotty was still a baby, my husband, Dick, and I dug into our meager Christmas fund to buy a dime store angel for the top of our tree. Esthetically, she was no prize: the plastic wings were lopsided, the gaudy robes painted haphazardly, the reds splashing over into the blues and purples. At night, though, she underwent a mysterious change—the light glowing from inside her robes softened the colors and her golden hair shone with the aura of a halo.

For six years she had the place of honor at the top of our tree. For six years, as in most families, Christmas was a time to be especially grateful for the wonderful gifts of God.

And then, in the seventh year, as summer enfolded us in her warm lethargy, I became aware of a new life gently stirring beneath my heart. Of all God's gifts this seemed the culmination, for we had long prayed for another child. I came home from the doctor's office and plunged straight into plans for a mood-setting dinner.

That evening when Dick walked in, candles flickered on the table and the children took their places, self-conscious in Sunday clothes "when it's just Wednesday!"

"Oh-oh," he grinned, "Mother's up to something—one of those special dinners again." I smiled and waited till halfway through the meal to make the announcement. But I got no further than the first informative sentence.

"You mean we're gonna have a baby?" squealed Miriam. Milk overturned and chairs clattered. Doors slammed and Dick and I were alone with our happiness while our three small Paul Reveres galloped wildly over the neighborhood shouting their news to everyone within lung distance.

Summer and fall sped by as we turned the spare room into a nursery and scraped and repainted baby furniture. December came again; once more we were on the verge of Christmas. Then one morning, eight weeks too soon for our new nursery to be occupied, I was rushed to the hospital.

Shortly past noon our four-pound son was born. Still groggy from the anesthetic, I was wheeled—bed and all—to the nursery to view Kirk Steven through an incubator porthole. Dick silently squeezed my hand while we absorbed the doctor's account of the dangers Kirk would have to overcome in order to survive. Added to his prematurity was the urgency for a complete blood exchange to offset RH problems.

All that long afternoon Dick and I prayed desperately that our son's life be spared. It was evening when I awoke from an uneasy doze to find our minister standing by the bed. No word was spoken, but as he clasped my hand, I knew. Our little boy had lived less than 12 hours.

During the rest of that week in the hospital, grief and disbelief swept over me by turn. At last Dick came to take me home. He loaded my arms with a huge bouquet of red roses, but flowers can never fill arms that ache to hold a baby.

In the street outside I was astonished to see signs of Christmas everywhere: the decorated stores, the hurrying shoppers, the lights strung from every lamp post. I had forgotten the season. For the sake of the children at home, we agreed, we would go through the emotions. But it would be no more than that.

And so a few days later Dick bought a tree and mechanically I joined him and the children in draping tinsel and hanging glass balls from the branches. Last of all, on the very top, went the forlorn dime store angel. Then Dick flipped the switch and again she was beautiful. Scotty gazed upward for a moment, then said softly, "Daddy, this year we have a *real* angel, don't we? The one God gave us."

And Dick and I, in our poverty, were going to give Christmas to our children—forgetting that it is always we who receive it from them! For, of course, God was the reality in tragedy as He had been in our joys, the unchanging Joy at the heart of all things. Scotty's words were for me like the light streaming now from the plastic angel, transforming what was poor and ugly on the surface into glory.

Tornado!

Charlotte Hale Smith

ON THE DAY before Christmas two years ago, the pastures of River Bend Farm near Covington, Georgia, were lush-green with winter rye grass. There, lording castle-like over 700 neat acres, was the dairy barn, two-stories high and large enough for the herd of 65 Holsteins on the ground floor, tons of stored hay and feed on the second. This was what River Bend Farm was like on the day before Christmas. On Christmas morning, the rye grass was still lush-green, but there was no barn; there was little left of the herd of Holsteins.

On the night which remembers Christ's birth, a ghostly tornado swirled through the Georgia countryside delivering not birth but destruction and death. The tornado was ghostly because no one at River Bend Farm saw it or felt its true havoc.

At five a.m. that Christmas morning, the Polk brothers, J.T. Jr. and Charles, started out in their pick-up truck for their morning chores. The Polks, who owned River Bend Farm, were progressive farmers. They were much respected in the area as good men and as good farmers. Over the years they had improved their land, and their herd had maintained one of the best production and quality records in the state. Both men—the very tall, tanned, laconic J.T. and the younger, smaller, boyish and fast-moving Charles—had a love for farming. This love showed itself in unexpected ways, like the affectionate names they had for each one of their many cows.

But this morning they sensed that something was wrong. It was still dark; the morning was unusually warm; the fog, thick as cream.

"Look, Charlie, last night's wind tore down the fence," J.T. said.

"Electric line's down too," Charles said, alarmed. "Get a flashlight and help me find the cows."

Then they heard the lowing in the distance; deep, frightened sounds of distress. The brothers dashed through the fog only to stop, unbelieving. What had been an enormous barn was now a grotesquely flattened mass of splintered wood.

"The cows! Look for the cows!" J.T. yelled as he lunged off toward the pasture, hoping the animals hadn't escaped through the broken fence.

It was Charles who recognized the worst. "Come back, J.T." he screamed. "The cows are *in* the barn!"

They didn't stop to think. They rushed in and started pulling bales of hay off the cows which were still alive. Other cows lay dead, twisted and crushed beneath the wreckage, suffocated by the 200 tons of hay that had fallen on them.

Once the brothers recognized the impossible task that faced them, they ran to the milking barn, called Civil Defense authorities, then raced back to their animals.

And soon, help came. Neighbors. Trucks. The implement company in nearby Covington sent two bulldozers; a neighbor arrived with a third. By daybreak the pastures and drives swarmed with people. Some came to watch, most stayed to work. When the Polks' driveway filled with trucks and machinery, friends cut the barbed wire to make new access. A state patrolman assumed traffic duty.

By afternoon, J.T. and Charles were in a daze, but they and nearly a hundred volunteers kept working, forgetting their Christmas stockings and the turkeys that would have to go in the ovens another day. The bulldozers dug in and pushed the debris aside, veterinarians ministered to injured animals, farmers loaded salvaged hay onto waiting trucks. The town's two hardware stores opened and distributed work gloves, pitchforks and shovels. Someone drove a haybaler to the scene and men retrieved scattered hay, rebaled it, loaded it aboard trucks.

By nightfall, River Bend Farm was neat again; there was a foundation dug and ready for a new barn. Exhausted, indescribably grateful, the brothers went home. Grateful they were, but beaten down. They had lost 47 cows. They faced a desperate future.

But the Polks had not reckoned fully with their neighbors. The community rallied even after Christmas had passed. They started bringing cows, one or two at a time, as gifts from farmers nearby and across the state. Mennonite farmers from Montezuma, Georgia—men utterly unknown to Covington farmers—brought 13 Holsteins, all top-quality milk cows, all gifts. And a fine Holstein costs $350 or more.

Other people gave money. Friends contributed $50, $100; one man gave $1,000. Fellow dairymen raised nearly $4,000 and there were people they didn't know who sent smaller sums from far across the United States.

Good deeds multiplied. A farm equipment firm replaced ruined implements at cost. Farmers donated feed, neighbors helped raise a new barn from materials donated or bought at cost and the building contractor gave his skills.

The Polks' wives wrote thank-you letters to as many people as they could, then worried because they couldn't track down everyone who helped.

Within six weeks, River Bend Farm had resumed operations, falteringly. By spring, new calves frisked in the pastures, and by summer the farm had begun to beat its own production records.

Christmas. It is returning again as it does every year, as it does everywhere, finding people in sorrow, in joy, in the emptiness or fullness of life. It is finding no one the same as the year before. The

Polks this year are different from the year of the tornado. They are better for their neighbors; they have been filled with the meaning of brotherhood, the meaning which so much of the world forgets—or refuses to remember.

The Miracle of Christmas

The wonderment
in a small child's eyes,
The ageless awe
in the Christmas skies . . .

The nameless joy
that fills the air,
The throngs that kneel
in praise and prayer . . .

These are the things that make us know
That men may come
and men may go,
But none will
ever find a way
To banish Christ
From Christmas Day . . .

For with each child
there's born again
A Mystery that baffles men.

Helen Steiner Rice

Yuletide Is Not Always So Merry

Faith Baldwin

ONCE, NOT SO long ago, I spent Christmas in a hospital, but not as a patient. In Baltimore a child of mine had lain for several months and would for many more to follow. We had resigned ourselves to the fact that for the first time since their birth, all the children of this household would not be together under their own roof in Connecticut.

Always there has been a tree, and the stockings have been hung and a great scurrying about the house has begun long before the Eve. And for a number of years upon that Eve we have gone to sing carols around a community tree and to church afterwards and then home, where we put the gifts in their appointed places, and then retired, all, even the oldest among us, too excited to sleep. But this year would be different.

We said, "No tree at home. Only one, a little one in the hospital room," and we were sensible, I think. But I am not really sensible. I mourned in my heart, which was silly of me, for I had known half a century's procession of lighted trees. Yet it was not, you understand, the tree I was mourning. . . .

I think it was on December twenty-first—a tree came to our home and was set up where it always stands. For those who loved me had said to one another, "She shall have her tree. . . ."

So on that day, and that day only, for we would not see it again, the tree was trimmed for me and the gifts brought down. We opened them, those we had wrapped against this time, thinking to open them long after December twenty-first had come and gone. And we had a sort of special dinner; just three of us, that evening, and said to one another, "Merry Christmas." We were not merry.

When we set off for Baltimore, we were laden with luggage and boxes, with gifts for our little girl in the hospital; gifts which included her first fur coat, gray and soft as a cloud. And we also brought small things for one another and our stockings to hang so that we might wake in the hotel on Christmas Day and feel somewhat at home.

I do not recall whether or not it snowed that year in that city: I think so, but am not sure. I have a remembrance of grayness and cold. But I remember most vividly the hospital room and the radiance of spirit within it, a spirit which transcended the long, brutal pain. The spirit shook me, because it was where I had not expected it.

We went shopping in that city, the child's godmother, her twin brother and I. We bought the fragile things for her tree which we could not bring with us; we bought garlands for her windows and a tree. . . .

There was a marble fireplace in that old fashioned room and we hung her stocking there, put the tree on the hearth, trimmed it, and set the wreaths in place and the gifts all about. And all the spirit that is Christmas laughed at us from the high hospital bed, with its ugly arrangement of ropes and pulleys and weights.

We left her at nine o'clock on Christmas Eve and returned to our hotel and hung our own stockings over the mantel in the impersonal living room and went to bed.

In the morning we had the small packages we had saved for this occasion and placed the long-distance telephone calls to those we missed and still could reach, and went to the hospital. And the tree had a special significance, as did the crammed stockings, the gay wreaths and bright paper wrappings.

I remember that later I went down the corridor from which many doors led to pain or death or slow returning life. I walked into a telephone booth, closed the door, but even through the glass I could hear the nurses laughing, and so I looked out and saw him—my tall boy walking down the corridor modelling his sister's fur coat. And I thought of all the people over all the many years who had sat in this same booth and spoken into the little black mouth of the telephone and of the things they had said, desperate things or hopeful; tragic things or happy . . . on holidays like this.

We ate our Christmas dinner in the hotel that afternoon. I

remember only being astonished at the custom which I had encoun-
tered in that same dining room at Thanksgiving—of serving sauer-
kraut with turkey. Then we took two Christmas dinners to the
hospital, complete in every respect, for our girl and her nurse.

But most of all I remember, that every time we entered or left
the hospital we passed the gigantic, merciful figure of Christ with
outstretched arms which stands there to bring to the anxious human
heart the age-old assurance of life immortal and love enduring.

This was but one Christmas out of many. I recall the earliest in
my memory; it seems to be a tiny picture of a tree, of a sugar plum
and of a great phonograph with a morning glory horn and strange
sounds issuing from the box, the wax cylinders turning and turning. I remember another Christmas, when sick for home, I stood in
the brilliant sunlight of the sub-tropics and looked at the palm trees
and longed for snow and firs and the Christmas fragrance . . . never
stopping to think that the Child whose birthday we celebrate was
born under bright skies and with the speaking palms nearby.

In many homes Christmas is something people wish to forget
and cannot because of the symbols all about them; perhaps, at this
season some one loved has slipped away. . . . Perhaps, they say, "I
don't believe in Christmas." *Why?* For none has really gone from
the house he once inhabited or from the hearts dedicated to him.
And who does not "believe" in Christmas cannot believe in him-

self, for in each of us there abides the Spirit which *is* Christmas, the Spirit which is hope and joy and strength.

All one day not long ago I found myself thinking, "What is man, that Thou art mindful of him?" I awoke thinking this; I had slept with the question in my mind. Somehow, at Christmas it is given to us to know the answer. For whatever man is, or is not, he is created in his Maker's image and is by his Creator loved and forgiven.

I remember that years ago a friend sent me a war-time newspaper from New Zealand, telling of a group of refugees from torpedoed ships who were landed just before Christmas on a lonely island. I later wrote this story for one of the magazines; it was a true story about the wounded and the ill, about men, women and children, about fear and agony and loss. A story of heroism and humility. And a story of people who, from whatever means at hand, built an altar and robed their Priest in vestments of white calico and red twill procured at the native store, and who on the Eve of Christmas, carried lanterns through tropical groves heavy with fragrance, came, singing and marching to the altar, Catholic and Protestant alike, to celebrate the Mass and take Communion.

For Christmas can be celebrated everywhere; in a hospital room, under a palm tree, on a lost, lonely island and in the heart. For beyond the symbols and the tradition there is the Spirit, the year round Spirit . . . if we but seek its unfailing Source.

The Failure That
Helped Me Grow Up

Penny DeFore
with a few fond interruptions
by her actor-father Don DeFore

IT SEEMS HARD to believe that only two years ago I spent Christmas in a Korean orphanage. This was an experience I'll always remember.

Don DeFore speaking: *In this article, my 19-year-old daughter Penny tells the story of her 1960 trip to Korea as a starry-eyed teenager to work as a volunteer in an orphanage not far from Seoul. She tells it honestly and vividly, but modestly, I think. I suffer from no such bashfulness where Penny is concerned, and so with your permission I would like to break in occasionally with a comment of my own. All right, Penny, over to you. . . .*

The first thing I was aware of on that bleak Christmas morning two year ago was cold: biting, bone-chilling cold. I was sleeping in most of my clothes, including a heavy fleece-lined parka. When I opened my eyes and looked around the bare little room where I slept alone—no electricity, no running water, no fireplace, no radiators—I couldn't help contrasting my surroundings with the warmth and luxury I had known on other Christmases.

Seven thousand miles away, I knew, my mother and my father and my four younger brothers and sisters would be thinking about me, missing me. When I thought of them, I could feel tears of homesickness sting my eyes.

I was an American teenager in a Korean orphanage, and I was there by choice. For four years—ever since I was 13—I had been hoping to go to Korea, planning to go, pleading with my parents to let me go. The reason was simple—or seemed simple to me. I had been given so much that I wanted to give something back.

All my life I had had everything a girl could want: a wonderful family, friends, comfort, security, love. I took these privileges completely for granted until the day in 1956 when I went to visit my father on a movie set and was introduced to a group of war orphans from Korea.

The picture they were making was *Battle Hymn*, a story based on the experiences of Col. Dean Hess of the U.S. Air Force who founded a home for Korean children orphaned by the war. About 25 of these children were in the film, and I was appalled by the hardships they had endured.

Don DeFore speaking: *Penny told us then that some day she wanted to go to Korea and try to help these unfortunate people. In the meantime, she said, she was going to raise money for the orphanage. She did too: by selling cakes and cookies and by working in the restaurant I then owned in Disneyland. In four years, Penny earned more than $700 for the orphanage.*

What was more, she said she had a feeling that God wanted her to go to Korea. Her mother and I tried to talk her out of it, but if a child wants to be unselfish, wants to give herself, wants to help others, how long can parents stand in the way? Finally we gave in. Worried? Of course we were worried! Sending a 17-year-old 7,000 miles would worry any parent!

Christmas Day was no time to be thinking about the cold, or my homesickness. I jumped up (believe me, I didn't have much dressing to do!), took my Bible in one hand and the little Santa Claus puppet an inspired friend had given me back in California, and ran down the path to the buildings where more than 250 orphans shivered in dormitories even colder than my room.

We had a happy Christmas morning together, those orphans and I. They loved it when I made the Santa Claus puppet bow and clap his hands for them; the language barrier was no problem for old Santa! We sang Christmas carols, and had a Christmas dinner that was somewhat better than the usual menu of rice, or seaweed wrapped in rice. For a little while the spirit of Christmas seemed to prevail. But as the freezing dusk began to settle, I felt terribly discouraged.

It wasn't just homesickness. It was something more frightening than that. It was a feeling that had been growing stronger ever since my arrival. The feeling that for all my good intentions, for all my desire to help, I really was not welcome. I was an outsider with alien ideas, with standards and attitudes that were different and therefore dangerous. The officials of the orphanage did not like it when I tried to help some of the children with their chores. They were incensed when I protested the harsh punishment given some of the children whose crime was selling the rags they wore in order to buy a pitiful taste of candy.

Don DeFore speaking: *Truth was, Penny had entered another world, a world where cruelty was common, where life was cheap, where standards of honesty and morality were different from our own. For the first time in her life, our Penny was face to face with the problem of evil . . . and she was facing it all alone.*

Perhaps it was a reaction to the emotionalism of Christmas, perhaps it was just self-pity, but when I finally went back to my little room I was overwhelmed with loneliness and despair. I tried to pray. All my life I have found peace of mind and renewed strength in prayer. Now I asked God to help me overcome the hostility I felt around me, to make me so understanding and loving that all the barriers would melt away.

And right there, in the middle of my prayer, came a thought so shattering and terrifying that I couldn't go on. It was the thought that perhaps this whole endeavor was not God's will for me at all, that it was nothing more than the romantic desire of a self-centered child who craved excitement and the publicity. *You're not really following God's plan for you,* a voice said inside of me. *You're following your own.*

That was the thought, the grim and desolate thought, with which I ended Christmas. I blew out the candle and crawled into bed, and I'm afraid my pillow was pretty damp before I finally fell asleep.

Don DeFore speaking: *It is a frightening thing to lose your conviction that what you're doing has God's approval. But many great souls have lived through such a crisis. And I, myself, believe that on that freezing Christmas night, in that far-off place, our Penny ceased to be a child and became that lonely, doubting, hesitant, groping thing: an adult human being.*

In the days that followed, I kept trying to do the things I had come to do. I began to learn a few words of Korean. I played with the children, sang songs to them, taught them games. They were wonderful: shy at first, then more and more responsive. But still I could not seem to break through the wall that separated me from the adult Koreans.

One night, praying about my situation, I told the Lord that I no longer knew whether it was His will for me to be in Korea or not. I told Him that no matter how I tried I could not seem to please the people in authority. I told Him that I was unable to cope with the problem any longer, and so I was turning it over to Him. If He wanted me to stay in Korea, I would stay. If He wanted me to go, I would go.

Three days later a visitor came to the orphanage. It was Dr. Kenneth Scott, a missionary who ran the Church World Service clinic for crippled children in Seoul. How much he knew about my situation, I don't know, but he asked me gently if I would like to transfer to his clinic, work as a therapist there, and live with some American friends of his in Seoul who had a daughter my age. I was so moved by this answer to my prayer that I was speechless. All I could do was nod my head.

The children wept when I left, and so did I. A failure? Yes, it was a failure. My brave hopes were disappointed. I had come up against a closed door, and I could not get through. But I believe God was trying to teach me something. He was trying to teach me that it isn't always enough to have good intentions and missionary zeal. You also must be prepared to suffer defeat.

And I learned another thing. When God closes one door for you, He often opens another. The months I spent in Korea after leaving the orphanage were joyous, happy, useful ones. The Scotts taught me how to put braces on the crippled children, how to help them eat, play games, walk with parallel bars. It was astounding, really: as soon as I surrendered my problem to God, I found myself doing what I had come to Korea to do.

I'm back in this wonderful country, now, but I'll never forget those two months I spent in the orphanage. Not only did they help me grow up, but they strengthened my faith in God's goodness and patience. If you just seek to do His will, He'll help you do it. That's the lesson I learned in Korea two years ago. It was the Christmas I'll never forget.

Don DeFore speaking: *Penny is in college now, studying to be a nurse. She hopes to go back to Korea, someday, with all the skill and training that she can acquire. She's not discouraged by what she calls her failure. To fail, and to learn, and to try again . . . that's what God wants us to do, isn't it? We think so, Penny, her mother and I.*

IV

CHRISTMAS

A Time for Giving

Christmas is a time for giving,

The Wise Men brought their best,

But Christ showed that the gift of self

Will out-give all the rest.

The Gift That Lasts a Lifetime

Pearl S. Buck

WE WOKE suddenly and completely. It was four o'clock, the hour at which his father had always called him to get up and help with the milking. Strange how the habits of his youth still clung to him after 50 years! He had trained himself to turn over and go to sleep, but this morning because it was Christmas, he did not try to sleep.

Yet what was the magic of Christmas now? His childhood and youth were long past, his father and mother were dead, and his own children grown up and gone. He and his wife were alone.

Yesterday she had said, "Let's not trim the tree until tomorrow, Robert—I'm tired."

He had agreed, and the tree was still out in the yard.

He slipped back in time, as he did so easily nowadays. He was 15 years old and still on his father's farm. He loved his father. He had not known how much until one day a few days before Christmas, when he had overheard what his father was saying to his mother.

"Mary, I hate to call Rob in the mornings. He's growing so fast and he needs his sleep. I wish I could manage alone."

"Well, you can't, Adam." His mother's voice was brisk.

"I know," his father said slowly, "but I sure do hate to wake him."

When he heard these words, something in him woke: his father loved him! He had never thought of it before. He got up quicker after that, stumbling blind with sleep, and pulled on his clothes, his eyes tight shut, but he got up.

And then on the night before Christmas, that year when he was 15, he lay on his side and looked out of his attic window. He wished he had a better present for his father than a ten-cent store tie.

The stars were bright outside, and one star in particular was so bright that he wondered if it were really the Star of Bethlehem. "Dad," he had once asked, "what is a stable?"

"It's just a barn," his father had replied, "like ours."

Then Jesus had been born in a barn, and to a barn the shepherds and the Wise Men had come, bringing their Christmas gifts.

The thought struck him like a silver dagger. Why should he not give his father a special gift? He could get up early, earlier than four o'clock, and he could creep into the barn and get all the milking done. He'd do it alone—milk and clean up, and then when his father went in to start the milking, he'd see it all done. And he would know who had done it.

He must have waked 20 times during the night. At a quarter to three he got up and put on his clothes. He crept downstairs, careful of the creaky boards, and let himself out. A big star hung low over the barn roof, a reddish gold. The cows looked at him, sleepy and surprised.

He had never milked all alone before, but it seemed almost easy. He kept thinking about his father's surprise. He smiled and milked steadily, two strong streams rushing into the pail, frothing and fragrant. The cows were still surprised but acquiescent. For once they were behaving well, as though they knew it was Christmas.

The task went more easily than he had ever known it to before. Milking for once was not a chore. It was something else, a gift to his father who loved him.

Back in his room he had only a minute to pull off his clothes in the darkness and jump into bed, for he heard his father up. He put the covers over his head to silence his quick breathing. The door opened.

"Rob!" his father called. "We have to get up, son, even if it is Christmas."

"Aw-right," he said sleepily.

"I'll go on out," his father said. "I'll get things started."

The door closed and he lay still, laughing to himself. The minutes were endless—ten, fifteen, he did not know how many—and he heard his father's footsteps again.

"Rob!"

"Yes, Dad—"

"You son of a—" His father was laughing, a queer sobbing sort of a laugh. "Thought you'd fool me, did you?"

"It's for Christmas, Dad!"

His father sat on the bed and clutched him in a great hug. It was dark and they could not see each other's faces.

"Son, I thank you. Nobody ever did a nicer thing—"

"Oh, Dad." He did not know what to say. His heart was bursting with love.

"Well, I reckon I can go back to bed," his father said after a moment. "No, listen—the little ones are waking up. Come to think of it, son, I've never seen you children when you first saw the Christmas tree. I was always in the barn. Come on!"

He got up and pulled on his clothes again and they went down to the Christmas tree, and soon the sun was creeping up to where the star had been. Oh, what a Christmas, and how his heart had nearly burst again with shyness and pride as his father told his mother and made the younger children listen about how he, Rob, had got up all by himself.

"The best Christmas gift I have ever had, and I'll remember it, son, every year on Christmas morning, so long as I live . . ."

They had both remembered it, and now that his father was dead he remembered it alone: that blessed Christmas dawn when, alone with the cows in the barn, he had made his first gift of true love.

On an impulse, he got up out of bed and put on his slippers and bathrobe and went softly upstairs to the attic and found the box of Christmas-tree decorations. He took them downstairs into the living room. Then he brought in the tree. It was a little one—they had not had a big tree since the children went away—but he set it in the holder and put it in the middle of the long table under the window. Then carefully he began to trim it.

It was done very soon, the time passing as quickly as it had that morning long ago in the barn. He went to his library and fetched the little box that contained his special gift to his wife, a star of diamonds, not large but dainty in design. He tied the gift on the tree and then stood back. It was pretty, very pretty, and she would be surprised.

But he was not satisfied. He wanted to tell her—to tell her how much he loved her. It had been a long time since he had really told her, although he loved her in a very special way, much more than he ever had when they were young.

Ah, that was the true joy of life, the ability to love! He was quite sure that some people were genuinely unable to love anyone. But love was alive in him, alive because long ago it had been born in him when he knew his father loved him. That was it: love alone could waken love.

And he could give the gift again and again. This morning, this blessed Christmas morning, he would give it to his beloved wife. He could write it down in a letter for her to read and keep forever. He went to his desk and began his love letter to his wife: *My dearest love* . . .

Then he put out the light and went tiptoeing up the stairs. The star in the sky was gone, and the first rays of the sun were gleaming in the sky. Such a happy, happy Christmas!

A Gift of the Heart

Norman Vincent Peale

NEW YORK CITY, where I live, is impressive at any time, but as Christmas approaches it's overwhelming. Store windows blaze with lights and color, furs and jewels. Golden angels, 40 feet tall, hover over Fifth Avenue. Wealth, power, opulence . . . nothing in the world can match this fabulous display.

Through the gleaming canyons, people hurry to find last-minute gifts. Money seems to be no problem. If there's a problem, it's that the recipients so often have everything they need or want that it's hard to find anything suitable, anything that will really say, "I love you."

Last December, as Christ's birthday drew near, a stranger was faced with just that problem. She had come from Switzerland to live in an American home and perfect her English. In return, she was willing to act as secretary, mind the grandchildren, do anything she was asked. She was just a girl in her late teens. Her name was Ursula.

One of the tasks her employers gave Ursula was keeping track of Christmas presents as they arrived. There were many, and all would require acknowledgment. Ursula kept a faithful record, but with a growing sense of concern. She was grateful to her American friends; she wanted to show her gratitude by giving them a Christmas present. But nothing that she could buy with her small allowance could compare with the gifts she was recording daily. Besides, even without these gifts, it seemed to her that her employers already had everything.

At night from her window Ursula could see the snowy expanse of Central Park and beyond it the jagged skyline of the city. Far below, taxis hooted and the traffic lights winked red and green. It was so different from the silent majesty of the Alps that at times she had to blink back tears of the homesickness she was careful never to show. It was in the solitude of her little room, a few days before Christmas, that her secret idea came to Ursula.

It was almost as if a voice spoke clearly, inside her head. "It's true," said the voice, "that many people in this city have much more than you do. But surely there are many who have far less. If you will think about this, you may find a solution to what's troubling you."

Ursula thought long and hard. Finally on her day off, which was Christmas Eve, she went to a large department store. She moved slowly along the crowded aisles, selecting and rejecting things in her mind. At last she bought something and had it wrapped in gaily colored paper. She went out into the gray twilight and looked helplessly around. Finally, she went up to a doorman, resplendent in blue and gold. "Excuse, please," she said in her hesitant English, "can you tell me where to find a poor street?"

"A poor street, Miss?" said the puzzled man.

"Yes, a very poor street. The poorest in the city."

The doorman looked doubtful. "Well, you might try Harlem. Or down in the Village. Or the Lower East Side, maybe."

But these names meant nothing to Ursula. She thanked the doorman and walked along, threading her way through the stream of shoppers until she came to a tall policeman. "Please," she said, "can you direct me to a very poor street in . . . in Harlem?"

The policeman looked at her sharply and shook his head. "Harlem's no place for you, Miss." And he blew his whistle and sent the traffic swirling past.

Holding her package carefully, Ursula walked on, head bowed against the sharp wind. If a street looked poorer than the one she was on, she took it. But none seemed like the slums she had heard about. Once she stopped a woman, "Please, where do the very poor people live?" But the woman gave her a stare and hurried on.

Darkness came sifting from the sky. Ursula was cold and discouraged and afraid of becoming lost. She came to an intersection and stood forlornly on the corner. What she was trying to do suddenly seemed foolish, impulsive, absurd. Then, through the traffic's roar, she heard the cheerful tinkle of a bell. On the corner opposite, a Salvation Army man was making his traditional Christmas appeal.

At once Ursula felt better; the Salvation Army was a part of life in Switzerland too. Surely this man could tell her what she wanted to know. She waited for the light, then crossed over to him. "Can you help me? I'm looking for a baby. I have here a little present for the poorest baby I can find." And she held up the package with the green ribbon and the gaily colored paper.

Dressed in gloves and overcoat a size too big for him, he seemed a very ordinary man. But behind his steel-rimmed glasses his eyes were kind. He looked at Ursula and stopped ringing his bell. "What sort of present?" he asked.

"A little dress. For a small, poor baby. Do you know of one?"

"Oh, yes," he said. "Of more than one, I'm afraid."

"Is it far away? I could take a taxi, maybe?"

The Salvation Army man wrinkled his forehead. Finally he said, "It's almost six o'clock. My relief will show up then. If you want to wait, and if you can afford a dollar taxi ride, I'll take you to a family in my own neighborhood who needs just about everything."

"And they have a small baby?"

"A very small baby."

"Then," said Ursula joyfully, "I wait!"

The substitute bell-ringer came. A cruising taxi slowed. In its welcome warmth, Ursula told her new friend about herself, how she came to be in New York, what she was trying to do. He listened in silence, and the taxi driver listened too. When they reached their destination, the driver said, "Take your time, Miss. I'll wait for you."

On the sidewalk, Ursula stared up at the forbidding tenement, dark, decaying saturated with hopelessness. A gust of wind, iron-cold, stirred the refuse in the street and rattled the ashcans. "They live on the third floor," the Salvation Army man said. "Shall we go up?"

But Ursula shook her head. "They would try to thank me, and this is not from me." She pressed the package into his hand. "Take it up for me, please. Say it's from . . . from someone who had everything."

The taxi bore her swiftly back from dark streets to lighted ones, from misery to abundance. She tried to visualize the Salvation Army man climbing the stairs, the knock, the explanation, the package being opened, the dress on the baby. It was hard to do.

Arriving at the apartment house on Fifth Avenue where she lived, she fumbled in her purse. But the driver flicked the flag up. "No charge, Miss."

"No charge?" echoed Ursula, bewildered.

"Don't worry," the driver said, "I've been paid." He smiled at her and drove away.

Ursula was up early the next day. She set the table with special care. By the time she had finished, the family was awake, and there was all the excitement and laughter of Christmas morning. Soon the living room was a sea of gay discarded wrappings. Ursula thanked everyone for the presents she received. Finally, when there was a lull, she began to explain hesitantly why there seemed to be none from her. She told about going to the department store. She told about the Salvation Army man. She told about the taxi driver. When she finished, there was a long silence. No one seemed to trust himself to speak. "So you see," said Ursula, "I try to do a kindness in your name. And this is my Christmas present to you. . . ."

How do I happen to know all this? I know it because ours was the home where Ursula lived. Ours was the Christmas she shared. We were like many Americans, so richly blessed that to this child from across the sea there seemed to be nothing she could add to the material things we already had. And so she offered something of far greater value: a gift of the heart, an act of kindness carried out in our name.

Strange, isn't it? A shy Swiss girl, alone in a great impersonal city. You would think that nothing she could do would affect anyone. And yet, by trying to give away love, she brought the true spirit of Christmas into our lives, the spirit of selfless giving. That was Ursula's secret—and she shared it with us all.

Christmas Bells

I heard the bells on Christmas Day,
Their old familiar carols play,
And wild and sweet the words repeat
Of peace on earth, good will to men.

I thought how, as the day had come,
The belfries of a Christendom
Had rolled along th' unbroken song
Of peace on earth, good will to men.

And in despair I bowed my head;
"There is no peace on earth," I said,
"For hate is strong, and mocks the song,
Of peace on earth, good will to men."

Then pealed the bells, more loud and deep:
"God is not dead, nor doth He sleep;
The wrong shall fail, the right prevail,
With peace on earth, good will to men."

Till, ringing, singing, on its way,
The world revolved from night to day
A voice, a chime, a chant sublime,
Of peace on earth, good will to men.

Henry W. Longfellow

Long Walk Part of Gift

Gerald Horton Bath

THE AFRICAN BOY listened carefully as the teacher explained why it is that Christians give presents to each other on Christmas day. "The gift is an expression of our joy over the birth of Jesus and our friendship for each other," she said.

When Christmas day came, the boy brought the teacher a sea shell of lustrous beauty. "Where did you ever find such a beautiful shell?" the teacher asked as she gently fingered the gift.

The youth told her that there was only one spot where such extraordinary shells could be found. When he named the place, a certain bay several miles away, the teacher was left speechless.

"Why . . . why, it's gorgeous . . . wonderful, but you shouldn't have gone all that way to get a gift for me."

His eyes brightening, the boy answered, "Long walk part of gift."

He's Straightest When He Stoops

Thomas J. Fleming

WHO ARE THE loneliest people at Christmas time? An asphalt salesman by the name of Dan Vinson asked himself this question several years ago. At first he decided that men and women in our prisons must be the loneliest people during the Christmas season. But, on thinking deeper, he came to the conclusion that the children of prisoners must be even lonelier. The result was a unique project.

Since 1943, Dan Vinson, of Oklahoma City, has sent out millions of Christmas presents to these kids without accepting a single cash contribution.

"We haven't done a thing until we give a part of ourselves," Vinson says. And that is what he asks—and receives—from hundreds of people in all walks of life. Working in barns, cellars and attics, Vinson's volunteers sort and package well over a million toys each year, which have been donated by businessmen everywhere.

The children who benefit have never heard of Dan Vinson; he does not want them to know he exists.

"A kid wants a Christmas present from someone he loves," Vinson says. "That's our basic idea."

Each year Vinson visits and corresponds with thousands of convicts and wardens, who have heard of him by word of mouth alone. Vinson sends each man a list of twenty-one toys. The imprisoned father checks the ones he wants, volunteers package the selections and mail them to the father, who re-addresses the package to his child. The present, then, is actually from the child's father.

V

CHRISTMAS

A Time for Understanding

Christmas is a time for understanding

People and customs throughout the world,

When for all-too-brief a season,

The banner of peace is unfurled.

Albert Schweitzer's Jungle Christmas

Glenn Kittler

WHEN CHRISTMAS comes to Albert Schweitzer's mission at Lambaréné, the Ogowe River runs at floodtide. Heavy rains have fallen in the Belgian Congo for almost a month, and there is at least another month of them ahead. Along the shores of the river, bursts of jungle flowers serve as landmarks, pointing to everyone's goal: the concrete steps which are the landing pier of the Albert Schweitzer Hospital.

All year the hospital is the center of heavy river traffic: the sick arriving, the cured going home to their distant villages. The morning I came to Lambaréné, fleets of the small dugouts clustered around the pier. Nearby, resting against a big rock, was Dr. Schweitzer, watching, waiting.

For more than 40 years Dr. Schweitzer has made his early morning visit to the river, welcoming patients and dispatching them, quickly and gently, to the clinic, surgery, the leper colony. As many as 250 sick arrive at Lambaréné in a single morning, some coming from 500 miles away—a fortnight's journey in Equatorial Africa.

Schweitzer once said, "I have come to Africa to help rectify some of the evils the white man has inflicted upon his black brother."

This he has done through a lifetime of healing bodies and souls. People are aware that there is something special about this place, and it seems most obvious at Christmas.

A Lambaréné Christmas starts many weeks before December 25. Gifts from European and American friends have a long trip, across oceans, slowly up the Ogowe from Port Gentil or perhaps by small plane from Brazzaville; there is no other way to reach the hospital. Once there, gifts must be carefully and constantly guarded against moisture, fungi, ants, even from birds. The gifts that survive these multiple hazards of travel and of the jungle are all the more treasured.

But, understandably, they are not so treasured as the gifts the staff itself exchanges. Some 25 lay missionaries—mostly Europeans and, because of a hospital's needs, mostly women—work with Schweitzer. They receive no pay, only a vitally needed rest trip home every two years, and many refuse even this.

Mrs. Stella Obermann, matronly widow of a Dutch clergyman and mother of another, has been at Lambaréné almost ten years, and she told me, "A strict rule has always been that we must each make our Christmas gifts ourselves, from odds and ends we save all year."

Each staff member gives—and receives—one gift; names are drawn
from Dr. Schweitzer's sun helmet weeks earlier. Then the secret
preparations start, if it is possible to keep a secret in the jungle. Out
of drawers come familiar wrappings and ribbons, familiar because
all have seen them before. They have been used for presents put at
a table place on birthday or anniversary mornings.

The Lambaréné staff has little time off, even at Christmas, and
so on Christmas Eve everyone is still at work far into the evening.
Dinner, as usual, is at 7:30, and the staff has just time to wash, fetch
their presents, and hurry to the refectory.

The dining hall stands on high ground, overlooking the long and
low hospital buildings, workshops, kitchens, and the administration
building, at one end of which is the humble room where Dr.
Schweitzer works and sleeps. You sense an immediate warmth in
the dining hall. Half a dozen small, green-shaded oil lamps line the
long table. The linen is snow-bright; the silver sparkles—a neatness
especially impressive compared to the jungle disorder outside.

At the far end of the room is a large floral decoration, typically
African: palm leaves, brilliant flowers, bright-colored fruit, vines,
branches from the rich green jungle shrubs. Small candles, guarded
by tin foil, glow throughout the display, and at the top is a tin foil
star. As the staff members enter, they put their gifts in front of the
decoration, then go to the table.

Dr. Schweitzer says grace; the meal begins. Schweitzer sits at the middle of the table. On his left is Mathilda Kottman, his first assistant, who came to Lambaréné in 1924. On his right is Mrs. Schweitzer, a small, lovely woman with a quick mind and a self-deprecating wit.

("Have you seen my lovely parrot?" Mrs. Schweitzer asked me. "I thought I had him trained, but he never talks when I want him to." And: "My husband and daughter have the same birthday. Mine is ten days later; I have always been behind everybody else.")

Because his chores keep him constantly moving, it is only at meals that you can study Dr. Schweitzer closely. Now 82, he is slightly stooped, yet he seems much taller than he is. He is well built; his step is heavy and firm; his hands, now gnarled from manual labor, still have their delicacy from the old days when he was the world's leading performer of Bach organ music.

His eyes are astonishingly blue, sometimes deep in thought, hidden by heavy brows, sometimes so bright with humor that you must smile when you look at him. I was with him one afternoon in the leper colony, a half mile from the hospital, where he was supervising a dozen Africans in the construction of a new ward. The work finished for the day, Schweitzer took off his hat, bowed majestically low to the Africans and said, "I thank you, gentlemen." The Africans laughed and returned the bow. I thought:

This is the man who at 21 was already an outstanding Protestant theologian, who since has written some of the most profound of spiritual books, and who was awarded the Nobel Peace Prize. He could have remained in Europe as one of its intellectual and religious leaders, but at 30 he gave up everything, took a degree in medicine, and went off to the hottest, wettest, most diseased part of Africa.

Schweitzer is merriest at Christmas Eve dinner. After the meal and a brief Bible reading, he plays the piano while others sing carols.

And then it's time to open presents, hand-made and heart-made by the devoted friends. Half of a well-known adage or famous quotation is attached to the present by the giver; the recipient must complete the saying before he can have his present. Stumblings, guesses, mistakes—all highlight the evening's merriment. Finally, after a prayer, the staff goes its separate ways—to bed or back to work.

Early Christmas morning finds everyone at his job; there are no holidays in an African hospital. Mid-morning, staff members give presents to their African helpers, and at noon gifts are distributed to the patients. A religious service follows, usually directed by a nurse. From the Catholic mission across the river, a priest comes to say Mass in the leper village.

By early afternoon, the compound is packed with Africans who have come many miles to spend Christmas with Dr. Schweitzer and his staff. He gives them presents sent to him by people from all over the world: clothes, cooking utensils, tools, toys for children, canned food, seeds for the next planting.

At last, when they are all gathered around him sitting on the ground, he reads them the Nativity story, then says:

"This is the story of God's love for us and the love we should have for each other. At one time when people were sick they were left at the roadside to die, but from Christ we learned that we must care for each other, sick or well, rich or poor, black or white. You must learn this and practice it. The doctors and nurses you see at the hospital have learned it and practice it. Christ is why they are here."

By the time refreshments are served and children perform a playlet of the birth of Christ, the day is well into evening and the staff hurries back to its jobs. After dinner, those who are free gather around for more carols, or simply to chat—soon it is late and time for bed.

And then it is morning again, another day, with everyone up at dawn and at his work, caring for the sick and the poor. Thus, for Dr. Albert Schweitzer and his staff, each one a true missionary, every day is rich with opportunities to demonstrate the charity of Christ's birthday. That is why they are there.

Undelivered Gifts

Wayne Montgomery

HAVE YOU ever had the experience of *almost not doing* an act of thoughtfulness or charity—only to discover later that without this action on your part a very important experience would not have happened to someone else?

Whenever I am tempted to be lazy or indifferent in this way, I inevitably think back to that Christmas in Korea, in 1951.

It was late afternoon on December 24. After a cold, miserable ride by truck in the snow, I was back at our Command Post. Shedding wet clothing, I relaxed on a cot and dozed off. A young soldier came in and in my sleep-fogged condition I heard him say to the clerk, "I wish I could talk to the Sergeant about this."

"Go ahead," I mumbled, "I'm not asleep."

The soldier then told me about a group of Korean civilians four miles to the north who had been forced to leave their burning village. The group included one woman ready to give birth. His information had come from a Korean boy who said these people badly needed help.

My first inner reaction was: how could we ever find the refugees in this snow? Besides, I was dead tired. Yet something told me we should try.

"Go get Crall, Pringle and Graff," I said to the clerk. When these soldiers arrived I told them my plan, and they agreed to accompany me. We gathered together some food and blankets; then I saw the box of Christmas packages in the corner of the office. They were presents sent over from charity organizations in the States. We collected an armful of packages and started out by jeep.

After driving several miles, the snow became so blinding that we decided to approach the village by foot. After what seemed like hours, we came to an abandoned Mission.

The roof was gone, but the walls were intact. We built a fire in the fireplace, wondering what to do next. Graff opened one of the Christmas packages in which he found some small, artificial Christmas trees and candles. These he placed on the mantel of the fireplace.

I knew it made no sense to go on in this blizzard. We finally decided to leave the food, blankets and presents there in the Mission in the hope that some needy people would find them. Then we groped our way back to the Command Post.

In April, 1952, I was wounded in action and taken to the hospital at Won Ju. One afternoon while basking in the sun, a Korean

119

boy joined me. He was a talkative lad and I only half listened as he rambled on.

Then he began to tell me a story that literally made me jump from my chair. After he finished, I took the boy to our chaplain; he helped me find an elder of the local Korean church who verified the boy's story.

"Yes, it was a true miracle—an act of God," the Korean church-man said. Then he told how on the previous Christmas Eve he was one of a group of Korean civilians who had been wandering about the countryside for days after North Korean soldiers had burned their village. They were nearly starved when they arrived at an old Mission. A pregnant woman in their group was in desperate condition.

"As we approached the Mission, we saw smoke coming from the chimney," the Korean said. "We feared that North Korean soldiers were there, but decided to go in anyway. To our relief, the Mission was empty. But, lo and behold, there were candles on the mantel, along with little trees! There were blankets and boxes of food and presents! It was a miracle!"

The old man's eyes filled with tears as he described how they all got down on their knees and thanked God for their deliverance. They made a bed for the pregnant woman and built a little shelter over her. There was plenty of wood to burn and food to eat and they were comfortable for the first time in weeks. It was Christmas Eve.

"The baby was born on Christmas Day," the man said. He paused. "The situation couldn't have been too different from that other Birth years ago."

On the following morning American soldiers rescued the Koreans, who later became the nucleus of a Christian church in the village where I was recuperating.

You just never know when you have a special role to play in one of God's miracles.

Christmas Promise

Whoever on the night of the
Celebration of the Birth of Christ
Carries warm water and a sleeping mat
To a weary stranger,
Provides wood from his own fire
For a helpless neighbor,
Takes medicine to one
Sick with malaria,

Gives food to children
Who are thin and hungry,
Provides a torch for a traveler
In the dark forest,
Visits a timid friend
Who would like to know about Christ,
Whoever does these things
Will receive gifts of happiness
Greater than that of welcoming a son
Returning after a long absence,
And though he live to be so old
That he must be helped into his hammock,
And though his family and friends all die
So that he stands as a trunk stripped of branches,
Yet life will be sweet for him,
And he will have peace,
As one whose rice harvest is great,
And who hears his neighbors
Praise the exploits of his youth.
So will you receive happiness
If you do these acts of love and service
On the night of the celebration of Christmas
The Birth of Christ.

The Christmas Song

Glenn Kittler

SADLY THE young pastor strolled through the snow-covered slopes above the village of Oberndof, Austria. In a few days it would be Christmas Eve, but Josef Mohr knew there would be no music in his church to herald the great event. The new organ had broken down.

Pausing, Pastor Mohr gazed at the scattered lights in the village below. The sight of the peaceful town, huddled warmly in the foothills, stirred his imagination. Surely it was on such a clear and quiet night as this that hosts of angels sang out the glorious news that the Saviour had been born.

The young cleric sighed heavily as he thought, "If only we here in Oberndof could celebrate the birth of Jesus with glorious music like the shepherds heard on that wonderful night!"

Standing there, his mind filled with visions of the first Christmas, Josef Mohr suddenly became aware that disappointment was fading from his heart; in its place surged a great joy. Vividly, he saw the manger, carved from a mountain side; he saw Mary and Joseph and the Child; he saw the strangers who had been attracted by the light of the great star. The image seemed to shape itself into the words of a poem.

The next day he showed the poem to Franz Gruber, the church organist, who said, "These words should be sung at Christmas. But what could we use for accompaniment? This?" Glumly, he held up his guitar.

The pastor replied, "Like Mary and Joseph in the stable, we must be content with what God provides for us."

Franz Gruber studied the poem, then softly strummed the melody that came to him. Next he put the words to the melody and sang them. When he finished, his soul was ablaze with its beauty.

On Christmas Eve, 1818, in a small Austrian village, the Oberndof choir, accompanied only by a guitar, sang for the first time the immortal hymn that begins, "Silent Night . . . Holy Night."

It Was That Night

It was that ethereal night
when a matchless star stood glowing in the East,
trailing a man, a woman, a burdened beast.

It was that incredible night
when an innkeeper became the first to say:
"I have no room for You this day."

It was that incomparable night
when Gabriel came ecstatic to the earth,
proclaiming glad tidings of a royal birth.

It was that immortal night
when a caring God reached gently down to lay,
His supreme gift, Love, upon the hay.

Fred Bauer

Prayer for Peace

Lord, make me an instrument of Thy peace.
Where there is hatred, let me sow love;
Where there is injury, pardon;
Where there is doubt, faith;
Where there is despair, hope;
Where there is darkness, light;
Where there is sadness, joy.

O Divine Master, grant that I may not so
much seek to be consoled, as to console;
To be understood, as to understand;
To be loved, as to love;
For it is in giving that we receive;
It is in pardoning that we are pardoned;
And it is in dying that we are born to
eternal life.

St. Francis of Assisi

VI

CHRISTMAS

A Time for Children

Christmas is a time for children

No matter what their age,

Spirit is the only ticket,

And heart the only gauge.

Sit Next to Me, Please

Robert H. Rockwell

IT WAS DARK when we arrived at the home for boys one evening
several years ago, but there was enough light to see the eager youngsters crowded on the porch and inside the doorway. Parentless boys,
or one-parent boys, they were. With avid interest they watched our
approach. But the 40-mile drive had been a tiring one in heavy traffic after a strenuous work day. Frankly I wasn't too happy about the
whole thing.

The trips were projects of our local Kiwanis Club. The last time
I had been asked to make this trip, I made an excuse, reasoning to
myself, "I send them a check each month. It isn't necessary to put
in an appearance at the banquets."

However, the time had come when excuses wouldn't do, and it
was embarrassing to refuse. I was a board member, and board members were expected to attend.

"Going to join us tomorrow night?" came the inevitable inquiry
from a friend.

"Why, yes, Bill. May I pick you up?"

I did. And here we were at the home.

"This always is a big night for the boys," Bill whispered as we walked to the porch. "It's almost embarrassing the way they enjoy our coming."

Two youngsters, age seven or eight, disengaged themselves from the other small fry and attached themselves to us.

"Will you be my company?" a solemn-eyed towhead pleaded uncertainly as he tugged at my coat.

"Sure thing, Fella!"

"My name's Jimmy. Jimmy Thompson. What's yours?"

I told him. Meanwhile the wide-eyed, evaluating gaze was unnerving. Emotions began to stir under the layers of fatigue.

"First time here, isn't it, Mister? Want me to show you around?"

"I'd like that."

He took me on a tour of inspection and importantly pointed out the gymnasium, the library, and his dorm—a narrow room lined with two rows of small iron beds.

"This is my very own wardrobe. See?" Pride was evident in the tone, but the boy seemed to be having some difficulty in breathing. Had we climbed that last flight of stairs too rapidly?

He opened the door of the not-very-wide metal cabinet and I was appalled at the insufficiency of his worldly goods. Guilty thoughts intruded as I mentally compared his inadequate possessions with the large, garment-filled closet and crammed toy chest of my own son.

"There's the dinner bell! We gotta hurry!" Jimmy exclaimed. "But let's not run, 'cause I've got asthma and I don't breath good when I hurry or get excited."

Then he stopped me for a moment. "Sit next to me at the table, willya, Mister? Please sit next to me!"

Of course I sat beside him. Bill was at the next table elbow-touching his small host. The guestless boys meanwhile turned their wistful glances continually to the tables boasting adult visitors.

By the time dinner was finished Jimmy and I were buddies. He had revealed that he was fatherless, that his mother worked in a supermarket and came each Sunday to take him home for the day, that he "wasn't much good" at athletics but that when he developed a "good breathin' chest" he'd like to become a ball player. Once when he thought I wasn't looking a slender hand lingered on my arm for a moment.

"This boy needs a father!" I anguished. "He's overflowing with love and there's no one to receive it!"

"Will you come again next month, Mister? If you do I'll save a place for you. Right next to me."

The pleading eyes were almost too much for me. I was having trouble with *my* breathing. Me! The smart guy who didn't want to give up an evening of TV to come here! Who thought generosity came through the checkbook. Why, this tyke had given me more in an hour than I could give to the home in a hundred years!

How selfish I was to consider money alone an adequate gift. Why does it take so long for most of us to learn that the real gift is of one's self?

"Promise you'll come next month?" The request was wheezed.

"Scout's honor," I replied. To myself, I said, "I'll be here, Jimmy. I wouldn't miss being here for anything, because you will be saving me a place. Right next to you."

Trouble at the Inn

Dina Donohue

FOR YEARS NOW whenever Christmas pageants are talked about in a certain little town in the Mid-west, someone is sure to mention the name of Wallace Purling. Wally's performance in one annual production of the Nativity play has slipped into the realm of legend. But the old-timers who were in the audience that night never tire of recalling exactly what happened.

Wally was nine that year and in the second grade, though he should have been in the fourth. Most people in town knew that he had difficulty in keeping up. He was big and clumsy, slow in movement and mind. Still, Wally was well liked by the other children in his class, all of whom were smaller than he, though the boys had trouble hiding their irritation when Wally would ask to play ball with them or any game, for that matter, in which winning was important.

Most often they'd find a way to keep him out but Wally would hang around anyway—not sulking, just hoping. He was always a helpful boy, a willing and smiling one, and the natural protector, paradoxically, of the underdog. Sometimes if the older boys chased the younger ones away, it would always be Wally who'd say, "Can't they stay? They're no bother."

Wally fancied the idea of being a shepherd with a flute in the Christmas pageant that year, but the play's director, Miss Lumbard, assigned him to a more important role. After all, she reasoned, the Innkeeper did not have too many lines, and Wally's size would make his refusal of lodging to Joseph more forceful.

And so it happened that the usual large, partisan audience gathered for the town's yearly extravaganza of crooks and crèches, of beards, crowns, halos and a whole stageful of squeaky voices. No one on stage or off was more caught up in the magic of the night than Wallace Purling. They said later that he stood in the wings and watched the performance with such fascination that from time to time Miss Lumbard had to make sure he didn't wander onstage before his cue.

Then the time came when Joseph appeared, slowly, tenderly guiding Mary to the door of the inn. Joseph knocked hard on the wooden door set into the painted backdrop. Wally the Innkeeper was there, waiting.

"What do you want?" Wally said, swinging the door open with a brusque gesture.

"We seek lodging."

"Seek it elsewhere." Wally looked straight ahead but spoke vigorously. "The inn is filled."

"Sir, we have asked everywhere in vain. We have traveled far and are very weary."

"There is no room in this inn for you." Wally looked properly stern.

"Please, good innkeeper, this is my wife, Mary. She is heavy with child and needs a place to rest. Surely you must have some small corner for her. She is so tired."

Now, for the first time, the Innkeeper relaxed his stiff stance and looked down at Mary. With that, there was a long pause, long enough to make the audience a bit tense with embarrassment.

"No! Begone!" the prompter whispered from the wings.

"No!" Wally repeated automatically. "Begone!"

Joseph sadly placed his arm around Mary and Mary laid her head upon her husband's shoulder and the two of them started to move away. The Innkeeper did not return inside his inn, however. Wally stood there in the doorway, watching the forlorn couple. His mouth was open, his brow creased with concern, his eyes filling unmistakably with tears.

And suddenly this Christmas pageant became different from others.

"Don't go, Joseph," Wally called out. "Bring Mary back." And Wallace Purling's face grew into a bright smile. "You can have *my* room."

Some people in town thought that the pageant had been ruined. Yet there were others—many, many others—who considered it the most Christmas of all Christmas pageants they had ever seen.

My Most Memorable Christmas

Catherine Marshall

WHY IS ONE Christmas more memorable than another?

It seldom has anything to do with material gifts. In fact, poor circumstances often bring out the creativity in a family.

But I think the most memorable Christmases are tied in somehow with family milestones: reunions, separations, births and, yes, even death. Perhaps that is why Christmas, 1960, stands out so vividly in my memory.

We spent that Christmas at Evergreen Farm in Lincoln, Virginia—the home of my parents. With us were my sister and her husband—Emmy and Harlow Hoskins—and their two girls, Lynn and Winifred. It meant a typical family occasion with our three children, Linda, Chester and Jeffrey, along with Peter John who was then a senior at Yale. Five children can make an old farmhouse ring with the yuletide spirit.

For our Christmas Eve service, Lynn and Linda had prepared an improvised altar before the living room fireplace. Jeffrey and

Winifred (the youngest grandchildren) lighted all the candles. Then with all of his family gathered around him, my father read Luke's incomparable account of the first Christmas. There was carol singing, with Chester and Winifred singing a duet, "Hark, the Herald Angels Sing," in their high piping voices. Then my mother, the story-teller of the family, gave us an old favorite, "Why the Chimes Rang." She made us see the ragged little boy creeping up that long cathedral aisle and slipping his gift onto the altar.

Then she said, "You know, I'd like to make a suggestion to the family. The floor underneath the tree in the den is piled high with gifts we're giving to one another. But we're celebrating Christ's birthday—not each other's. This is His time of year. What are we going to give to Jesus?"

The room began to hum with voices, comparing notes. But Mother went on, "Let's think about it for a few moments. Then we'll go around the circle and each of us will tell what gift he will lay on the altar for Christ's birthday."

Chester, age seven, crept close to his father for a whispered consultation. Then he said shyly, "What I'd like to give Jesus this year is not to lose my temper anymore."

Jeffrey, age four, who had been slow in night training, was delightfully specific. "I'll give Him my diapers."

Winifred said softly that she was going to give Jesus good grades in school. Len's was. "To be a better father, which means a gift of more patience."

And so it went . . . on around the group. Peter John's was short but significant. "What I want to give to Christ is a more dedicated life." I was to remember that statement five years later at the moment of his ordination into the Presbyterian ministry when he stood so straight and so tall and answered so resoundingly, "I do so believe . . . I do so promise . . ." Yet at Christmastime, 1960, the ministry was probably the last thing he expected to get into.

Then it was my father's turn. "I certainly don't want to inject too solemn a note into this," he said, "but somehow I know that this is the last Christmas I'll be sitting in this room with my family gathered around me like this."

We gasped and protested, but he would not be stopped. "No, I so much want to say this. I've had a most wonderful life. Long, long ago I gave my life to Christ. Though I've tried to serve Him, I've failed Him often. But He has blessed me with great riches—especially my family. I want to say this while you're all here. I may not have another chance. Even after I go on into the next life, I'll still be with you. And, of course, I'll be waiting for each one of you there."

There was love in his brown eyes—and tears in ours. No one said anything for a moment. Time seemed to stand still in the quiet room. Firelight and candlelight played on the children's faces as they looked at their grandfather, trying to grasp what he was saying. The fragrance of balsam and cedar was in the air. The old windowpanes reflected back the red glow of Christmas lights.

Father did leave this world four months later—on May 1st. His passing was like a benediction. It happened one afternoon as he sat quietly in a chair in the little village post office talking to some of his friends. His heart just stopped beating. That Christmas Eve he had known with a strange sureness that the time was close.

Every time I think of Father now, I can see that scene in the living room—like a jewel of a moment set in the ordinary moments that make up our days. For that brief time real values came clearly into focus: Father's gratitude for life; Mother's strong faith; my husband's quiet strength; my son's inner yearning momentarily shining through blurred youthful ambitions; the eager faces of children groping toward understanding and truth; the reality of the love of God as our thoughts focused on Him whose birth we were commemorating.

It was my most memorable Christmas.

She Kept Her Promise

John Markas

THE EXPERIENCE happened when I was 13 and seemed hardly worth telling anyone at the time. But now, ten years later, it stands above any other Christmas memory I have.

There were 118 customers on my paper route in Morganton, North Carolina. As Christmas drew near I began to nudge my customers into a "remember the paper boy" mood. I bought 118 cheap Christmas cards, signed them "Your friendly paper boy" and several days before Christmas inserted one card in each paper.

The results were quite satisfactory—in fact, almost spectacular. The standard reply was a dollar bill slipped into an envelope marked "paper boy."

Except for Mrs. Luke Woodbury, a widow known for her devoutness. Mrs. Woodbury was standing at the door when I arrived with her Christmas paper.

"I wanted to thank you personally, Johnny, for your card," she said. "It was a kind and thoughtful act to an old lady."

The warmth of her greeting made me feel a little uneasy.

"I haven't much to give you," she said handing me a few coins, "but I do want you to know this: I see you every day when you pass the house. Every day I will pray for you, Johnny. I will pray that God will help you and guide you wherever you go, whatever you do."

She put her hand on my shoulder, almost like a caress, and then went back into her house.

A 13-year-old is more inclined to be uncomfortable than moved by such an experience. I certainly didn't think too much about it at the time. Nor did I have any undue interest in religion.

In the years that followed I saw Mrs. Woodbury on a few occasions. She always smiled at me in a meaningful way. When I went to Duke University I forgot about Mrs. Woodbury until . . .

Until two years ago when the turning point in my life came at a Fellowship of Christian Athletes' conference. A perfunctory Christian until then, I stepped from the darkness of ordinary living into the brightness and joyousness of a new life with Christ at the center.

Soon after this experience I was giving a talk in Chattanooga in which I re-evaluated my life. I spoke about how lucky I was. For the truth of the matter is that I have had to work very hard for my "C" average in college. As for football, during my high school and early college years I had been short of both weight and talent. Yet somehow I was able to find within myself the extra strength or ability I needed to do what had to be done.

After church a lady told me:

"That was not luck; you've obviously had some people praying hard for you all this time."

This was a sudden new thought. My parents, of course. Their faith always had been strong.

And then I remembered Mrs. Woodbury—and her promise to pray for me. How much I owed her!

A few months ago I discovered that Mrs. Woodbury had entered a Home where she could get special care. As a tribute to her—and all the unselfish, thoughtful people who pray for others—I tell this story of what I now consider my most memorable Christmas.

A Boy's Finest Memory

Cecil B. DeMille

DURING THIS festive Christmas season, churches all over the country will overflow with worshipers. It wasn't always that way . . .

When I was a boy of ten, our community church, in order to stimulate interest among parishioners, decided to hold services every morning at 8 A.M. for a week. Since we couldn't afford a resident minister, one was acquired from the outside. I do not remember his name. But I shall never forget his strong, kindly face and his prominent red beard.

My father, who was very active in the church, sent me off one cold and rainy morning. I walked alone to the small, wooden sanctuary through a murky gloom. Upon arriving, I could see that no one was present but the red-bearded minister and me.

I was the congregation.

Embarrassed, I took a seat, wondering anxiously what he would do. The hour for the service arrived. Surely he would tell me politely to run along home.

With calm and solemn dignity the minister walked into the pulpit. Then he looked down on me and smiled—a smile of great warmth and sincerity. In the congregation sat a solitary child, but he commenced the service as if the church were crowded to the walls.

A ritual opened the services, followed by a reading lesson to which I gave the responses. Then the minister preached a short sermon. He talked earnestly to me—and to God. When it came time for the offering, he placed the collection plate on the altar railing. I walked up and dropped my nickel into the plate.

Then he did a beautiful thing. He came down to the altar to receive my offering. As he did this, he placed his hand on my head. I can still feel the thrill and sensation of his gentle touch. It won my belief and strengthened my faith. The spirit of truth was in the church with us that morning.

None of us can tell at what moment we step into a boy's life and by a demonstration of love and faith turn him in God's direction.

Hope for the New Year

Ring out, wild bells, to the wild sky,
The flying cloud, the frosty light:
The year is dying in the night;
Ring out, wild bells, and let him die.

Ring out a slowly dying cause,
And ancient forms of party strife;
Ring in the nobler modes of life,
With sweeter manners, purer laws.

Ring out false pride in place and blood,
The civic slander and the spite;
Ring in the love of truth and right,
Ring in the common love of good.

Ring out old shapes of foul disease;
Ring out the narrowing lust of gold;
Ring out the thousand wars of old,
Ring in the thousand years of peace.

Ring in the valiant man and free,
The larger heart, the kindlier hand;
Ring out the darkness of the land,
Ring in the Christ that is to be.

Alfred Tennyson

VII

CHRISTMAS

A Time for Learning

Christmas is a time for learning,

A time when new truths unfold,

And not-so-innocent children

Often teach the old.

Gold, Circumstance and Mud

Rex Knowles

IT WAS THE week before Christmas. I was baby-sitting with our
four older children while my wife took the baby for his check-up.
(Baby-sitting to me means reading the paper while the kids mess
up the house.)

Only that day I wasn't reading. I was fuming. On every page of
the paper, as I flicked angrily through them, gifts glittered and rein-
deer pranced, and I was told that there were only six more days in
which to rush out and buy what I couldn't afford and nobody needed.
What, I asked myself indignantly, did the glitter and the rush have
to do with the birth of Christ?

There was a knock on the door of the study where I had barri-
caded myself. Then Nancy's voice, "Daddy, we have a play to put
on. Do you want to see it?"

I didn't. But I had fatherly responsibilities so I followed her into
the living room. Right away I knew it was a Christmas play for at
the foot of the piano stool was a lighted flashlight wrapped in swaddling clothes lying in a shoe box.

Rex (age 6) came in wearing my bathrobe and carrying a mop handle. He sat on the stool, looked at the flashlight. Nancy (10) draped a sheet over her head, stood behind Rex and began, "I'm Mary and this boy is Joseph. Usually in this play Joseph stands up and Mary sits down. But Mary sitting down is taller than Joseph standing up so we thought it looked better this way."

Enter Trudy (4) at a full run. She never has learned to walk. There were pillowcases over her arms. She spread them wide and said only, "I'm an angel."

Then came Anne (8). I knew right away she represented a wise man. In the first place she moved like she was riding a camel (she had on her mother's high heels). And she was bedecked with all the jewelry available. On a pillow she carried three items, undoubtedly gold, frankincense, and myrrh.

She undulated across the room, bowed to the flashlight, to Mary, to Joseph, to the angel, and to me and then announced, "I am all three wise men. I bring precious gifts: gold, circumstance, and mud."

That was all. The play was over. I didn't laugh. I prayed. How near the truth Anne was! We come at Christmas burdened down with gold—with the showy gift and the tinsely tree. Under the circumstances we can do no other; circumstances of our time and place and custom. And it seems a bit like mud when we think of it.

But I looked at the shining faces of my children, as their audience of one applauded them, and remembered that a Child showed us how these things can be transformed. I remembered that this Child came into a material world and in so doing eternally blessed the material. He accepted the circumstances, imperfect and frustrating, into which He was born, and thereby infused them with the divine. And as for mud—to you and me it may be something to sweep off the rug, but to all children it is something to build with.

Children see so surely through the tinsel and the habit and the earthly, to the love which, in them all, strains for expression.

A Boy's Christmas Discovery

Charles E. Lesperance

WHEN MY SON Larry was six, I drove him through the city showing him dozens of Santas, explaining that they were either volunteers raising funds for the poor or they were on the payrolls of department stores to attract and amuse children.

Then I told him the meaning of Christmas as I understood it. "We celebrate Christmas," I said, "in honor of Jesus, who was born on that day, and we exchange gifts with people we love just as the Three Wise Men brought gifts to the Baby Jesus. Celebrating Christmas is a way of showing that we believe in God and that Jesus was His son. We go to church at Christmas to let God know that we believe."

Larry soberly accepted my explanation. But as Christmas approached, the joy seemed to have gone out of him. Deep down I sensed there had been something missing in my well-meaning attempt to explain that Santa was not the essence of Christmas.

On Christmas Eve our family went to the services at our church; I placed Larry next to me to hold him in case he fell asleep. The service had just begun when I felt him tug at my sleeve. I followed his gaze across the aisle.

There knelt an old man, his cheeks flushed from the cold night, his white beard still aglitter with snowflakes. Protruding from under his heavy overcoat were red pantaloons, tucked into shiny black boots. Dangling from his pocket was a red cap, complete with a big white tassel. His head was bowed, his eyes were closed, his lips moved in prayer.

I was about to lean over and give my explanation to Larry, but before I could speak, Larry looked up, and his expression of enraptured triumph silenced me.

"See, Daddy," he whispered, "Santa Claus believes, too!"

The Gift of a Child

Mary Ann Matthews

CHRISTMAS COMES at different times for me every year. I never know precisely when it will arrive or what will produce its spirit, but I can always be sure that it will happen.

Last year Christmas happened while I was visiting my parents in Conneaut, Ohio. The day was frightfully cold, with swirls of snow in the air, and I was looking out of the living room window of my folks' home which faces St. Mary's Church. Workmen had just finished constructing the annual nativity scene in the churchyard when school let out for the day. Children gathered excitedly around the crèche, but they didn't stay long; it was far too cold for lingering.

All the children hurried away—except for a tiny girl of about six. The wind lashed at her bare legs and caused her coat to fly open in the front, but she was oblivious of the weather. All her attention was riveted on the statues before her. Which one I couldn't tell. Was it Mary? The Baby? The animals? I wondered.

And then I saw her remove her blue woolen head scarf. The wind quickly knotted her hair into a wild tangle, but she didn't seem to notice that either. She had only one thought. Lovingly, she wrapped her scarf around the statue of Baby Jesus. After she had covered it, she patted the Baby and then kissed it on the cheek. Satisfied, she skipped on down the street, her hair frosted with tiny diamonds of ice.

Christmas had come once again.

Pattern of Love

Jack Smith

AS TOLD TO RAYMOND KNOWLES

I DIDN'T question Timmy, age nine, or his seven-year-old brother Billy about the brown wrapping paper they passed back and forth between them as we visited each store.

Every year at Christmastime, our Service Club takes the children from poor families in our town on a personally conducted shopping tour. I was assigned Timmy and Billy, whose father was out of work. After giving them the allotted $4 each, we began our trip. At different stores I made suggestions, but always their answer was a solemn shake of the head, no. Finally I asked, "Where would you suggest we look?"

"Could we go to a shoe store, Sir?" answered Timmy. "We'd like a pair of shoes for our Daddy so he can go to work."

In the shoe store the clerk asked what the boys wanted. Out came the brown paper. "We want a pair of work shoes to fit this foot," they said.

Billy explained that it was a pattern of their Daddy's foot. They had drawn it while he was asleep in a chair.

The clerk held the paper against a measuring stick, then walked away. Soon, he came with an open box. "Will these do?" he asked.

Timmy and Billy handled the shoes with great eagerness. "How much do they cost?" asked Billy.

Then Timmy saw the price on the box. "They're $16.95," he said in dismay. "We only have $8."

I looked at the clerk and he cleared his throat. "That's the regular price," he said, "but they're on sale; $3.98, today only."

Then, with shoes happily in hand the boys bought gifts for their mother and two little sisters. Not once did they think of themselves.

The day after Christmas the boys' father stopped me on the street. The new shoes were on his feet, gratitude was in his eyes. "I just thank Jesus for people who care," he said.

"And I thank Jesus for your two sons," I replied. "They taught me more about Christmas in one evening than I had learned in a lifetime."

The Winner

Glenn Kittler

THE NOISE was enough to make Father Bonaventure almost regret having given this party. "The wild Indians are certainly running true to form," he thought.

The children were indeed Indians—members of the Papago tribe, and this was their first Christmas party, given them by the Franciscan priests at the San Xavier Reservation Mission south of Tucson, Arizona.

One boy, Luis Pablo, was a special problem. He kept trying to take away prizes won by other boys.

"Luis!" Father said severely, "why can't you behave?"

"I want to win something," Luis complained.

"Then win something," said Father. "Don't steal it."

At the end of the party the children formed a line and to each Father presented a bag of hard candy. When eight-year-old Luis' turn came he asked, "Can I have three bags?"

"You cannot," said Father sternly. "One bag to each."

"But I mean empty bags."

"Oh! Well, why not?" Father gave Luis three bags and the boy left.

Later, alone in his office, the priest glanced out the window and saw Luis sitting on the school steps. He had three bags open beside him and, carefully, was dividing his candy into them. Then Father Bonaventure suddenly remembered: at home Luis had two brothers and a sister. They were too young to come to the Christmas party. So this was the reason . . .

The priest went to the party room and scooped the remaining candy into a large bag. It was to go to the Sisters, but he knew that they would not object to what he was about to do. Outside he gave the bag to Luis.

This Quiet Night

Hush,
The Baby sleeps
In the arms of His loving mother.
The night is still
And the beasts of the stable hover
Near in soundless adoration.

Hush,
The world's asleep
In the dreams of this loving Infant.
Our hearts are still
And the beasts of our minds take instant
Calm in boundless adoration.

Sleep, Child, sleep
Your sleep of purity.
Sleep, world, sleep
In God's security.

Rehobeth Billings

VIII

CHRISTMAS

A Time for Sharing

Christmas is a time for sharing,

A time for needy hands to clasp,

A time for stretching out in faith

With a reach that exceeds our grasp.

Holiday Candles

Betty Girling

THE MOST memorable Christmas in my life occurred many years ago when I was eleven. My father and mother had left Ohio to homestead in Nebraska. Our first winter there began bleak and cold and, above all, lonely. We had no neighbors. Once there'd been other homesteaders nearby but they'd moved before we came. Across the fields their cabin stood empty.

In Ohio we'd been used to friends and activity and going to church; but here we lived too far out and my father made the long trip into town only occasionally for supplies.

A few days before Christmas, Pa saddled our horse, Thunder, and rode off to town to get the candles he'd promised for our tree.

Shortly after he left Mother and I were surprised to see a team of horses approaching the empty farmhouse across the field. Soon we could see figures unloading furniture.

"Neighbors!" Mother cried, joyfully.

The next moment she had on her coat and was trudging across our snow crusted cornfields with a loaf of fresh baked bread. Soon Mother was back accompanied by a girl of my age.

"This is Sarah Goodman," she said.

Sarah and I looked at each other shyly. Then I found myself telling her all about the Christmas tree we were going to have when Pa got back from town.

Softly, Sarah said to me: "We're Jewish."

I'd never known a Jewish girl before. Suddenly I felt silly, babbling about trees and candles, and I was sorry for Sarah, not having any Christmas.

"Well, never mind," I told her, struck by a sudden thought, "you have special holidays too, I guess."

"Oh, yes, we have Hanukkah," she began eagerly. "That's our Feast of Lights . . ." she broke off and jumped to her feet. "Oh, with all the moving, we've forgotten! Why it's already . . ." she counted on her fingers, "it's the fifth day. And I don't even know where we packed the Menorah!" Then with a hasty good-by she ran out and across the fields to her own house.

Mother and I watched her go in surprise, wondering what a "Menorah" might be. Even as we watched it began to snow.

I stayed at the window all afternoon, peering into the white maelstrom. Faster and thicker the snow fell—till I couldn't see Mother's lilac bush a scarce five feet away.

At six Pa had not returned and Mother's face was grim. Here on the plains *blizzard* is a fearsome word. Hadn't they told us in town about the homesteader they found, last winter, frozen to death only four feet from his own barn door?

At 11:00, when Mother finally put me to bed, the blizzard was still raging and Pa had not returned.

At dawn the storm was over. Deep snowdrifts piled high around the house, but the sky was clearing. Mother was sitting in a chair, still waiting. Suddenly we heard shouts and we raced to the door.

Pushing through the drifts came father, Sarah Goodman and her parents. In they tramped. Soon we were all clustered around the kitchen stove, getting warm.

"It was a miracle," Pa said. "That's what it was, a miracle!"

While mother cooked breakfast Pa told us how he'd got lost in the storm. The road was completely obliterated, he could see nothing in the dark, and had to depend on the horse's instinct for guidance. But finally Thunder wouldn't go on.

"I was nearly frozen by then," Pa said. "So I jumped off the horse and started leading him, just to keep warm. For hours we floundered on. We'd work one way till the drifts got too deep, then turn and work another."

Pa knew he was pretty close to exhaustion when suddenly, through the swirling snow off to one side, he saw some tiny pinpoints of light.

"As I led Thunder toward those lights, I prayed they would still keep shining, and when I reached them I found myself at the Goodmans' cabin. There in the window was a great candlestick, like none I'd ever seen before. Nine candles it held, six of them lighted."

"That was our Menorah," said Sarah, "for Hanukkah, our Feast of Lights. I put it in the window."

"Then you saved Pa's life!"

"Not exactly," said Mr. Goodman, gently. "Sarah really put it on the window sill hoping you would see it and know that she was celebrating her holiday, at this time, like you will be keeping your Christmas."

Mother set us down to breakfast just then and Pa bowed his head, saying: "Almighty God, we thank Thee for the blessings of this season."

The Family in the Parking Lot

Norman Spray

HAVE YOU ever looked at the holidays with a cold and practical eye and then talked yourself into believing that Christmas was not worth all the trouble?

I was making just such a cold and practical appraisal as the Christmas of 1956 approached. On December 11 of that year, another blue-and-purple norther was whistling through our town of Bedford, Texas, and I was in a fittingly icy mood as I drove to work that cold and bleak morning.

I knew that very morning I faced a deadline on the Christmas issue of the employee news magazine I edited for the Bell Helicopter Company. So far the issue was a mess. Little copy had been written and, worse, my idea well was dry.

"Why should we bother with a Christmas issue anyway?" I asked myself. "In today's busy world who really cares?" Besides, who was I to write a sermon on peace and goodwill to interest men and women who built helicopters? After all, we were publishing a line of communication between management and employees—not a Sunday-school bulletin.

I drove up to the Bell plant. A car was stopped ahead of me, and the driver was talking to the guard at the gate. Beside the driver sat a dark-haired young woman, and in the back, wedged in among a seatful of battered old suitcases, sat a shaggy-haired little boy holding a puppy. The guard pointed directions, and the car drove off toward the visitors parking lot. I didn't know it then, but before the day was out, that car and those people would become important to me.

The driver of that car was Frank Gates, and his wife of four years, Eugenia, sat beside him while their three-year-old son, Frank, Jr., sat in the back. Frank was a logger. He had been working up in Montana, but logging operations had closed down for the winter a week before and Frank had lost his job—again.

He had heard that in Texas he might be able to get year-round work, and so they had loaded their belongings into the old car and headed south. They ate lightly and at night slept in the car because they had barely enough money just for gasoline.

The family had arrived in Fort Worth on the evening of December 10, penniless, bone-tired and famished. Frank had gone to a construction company which happened to be building a new addition to our Bell plant, and they had hired him immediately as a laborer at $1 an hour. That wasn't much, even in those days—unless you'd just arrived from Montana with nothing at all.

"This is it, honey," Frank had said to Eugenia, elated. "From now on, things are going to be better." On that blustery night they had shared a quart of milk and bedded down in the car in high spirits.

"I'm a new man on the construction job out here," Frank had just said to the guard when I first saw him. "Can I park around here?" The guard had no idea that Frank wanted to park his car *and* his family there for the entire day.

At midmorning, the guard captain at plant-security headquarters got a phone call from the gate guard. "A woman and a kid are out here in an old car. They've been here all morning."

The captain and a guard lieutenant went out to speak to the young mother. She looked tired—very tired. "Why," the lieutenant asked, "are you staying in the car?"

Eugenia explained, "We're going to try to find a place when my husband gets off work today."

The two officers both knew that company rules forbade her staying there in the parking lot, so they arranged for Eugenia to park at a service-station lot across the street. While the move was being made they overheard the boy plead, "I'm hungry, Mommy."

Back at the guard office the two security officers told what had happened. It was then that two other guards suggested that they buy lunch for the mother and son. Instantly, $3 was on the table.

One guard carried the money to the plant cafeteria. When the cafeteria manager heard the story, he heaped two plates. "It's on the house," he said.

Eugenia was grateful when the guard handed her the plates, but when he insisted she take the $3 besides, she became emotional. "Thank you very much," she said, her voice breaking. "But we'll pay you back."

The guard returned to the front-gate guard station. "These are good people, just down on their luck," he told the other guards. "We ought to help them if we can."

The captain and lieutenant went to talk to Frank Gates. "This young fellow's not about to ask anybody for help," the captain said afterward. "All he wants is a chance."

"Trouble is, he won't get paid for two weeks," the lieutenant added.

The last comment left the guards silent. Two weeks is a long time to camp out in a car.

There was a plant rule against employee solicitation, a rule the guards were responsible for enforcing. But in any plant there is a shadowy information network, the grapevine. And at Bell that day, word of the mother's plight swept through the plant. The guards' first act of kindness was multiplied as secretaries and production workers began building a kitty to help a couple they had only heard about.

And that was when I heard about the Gateses, only ten minutes before I was to meet with my boss to talk about the Christmas issue.

Mildly interested, I took a note pad and ambled out to the security office. By then someone had come up with the idea of offering the family some of the clothing that was being collected at the plant for Hungarian relief.

On Frank's lunch hour, the young logger and his family were escorted to the clothes collection point. Hesitantly, they picked a few items: a jacket for Frank, a pair of shoes and overalls for the boy. "This is all we'll need until we get started," said Eugenia. She was careful not to take too much from "those poor people in Hungary."

I went back to my desk and called my wife. I told her about the young Gates family. Barby's reaction was instantaneous—and practical.

"Meet me at their car," she said in the definite tone she reserves for times when she doesn't mean to be questioned. "I'm bringing that woman and her boy home with me."

I walked back to the front gate. A riveter from the factory strode up. "The boys around the plant want this to go to that woman and child out front," he told the guards. "Folks just heard about them and reached for their wallets." He laid $96 on the desk.

Nobody asked any questions—rules or no rules. Another guard, accompanied by the president of the union local, took the gift to Eugenia; I tagged along. There was no fancy speech as the union official said simply, "The folks in the plant want you to have this."

This time, the tired, disheveled Eugenia couldn't hold back the tears. She just sat there, stroking her son's puppy, letting the drops fall unashamedly.

Barby drove up. "I want you to come and visit me until your husband gets off work," Barby said.

Eugenia was hesitant, but she accepted. When Barby brought her back to the plant that afternoon at quitting time, she looked like a new woman, years younger, even radiant. She had napped and bathed and fixed her hair, and Frank Jr., was sparkling clean. She could hardly wait to rush into the arms of her husband.

"You people are wonderful," he said. "I can't say how wonderful. We'll pay you back. It'll take a little time, but we'll pay you back."

The next morning, Frank appeared on the job 30 minutes before starting time—clean-shaven, rested, the picture of a man with a future. He whistled merrily and strode briskly.

Everyone I met that day wore a cheery smile and had a pleasant greeting. It wasn't imagination—the plant had changed overnight into a friendlier, happier, better place. Suddenly Christmas was everywhere. Suddenly I believed again in its miracle.

In the course of one day I learned that Christmas can never be looked at properly with a cold and practical eye; its value cannot be measured that way. Frank Gates and his family had helped me find a story, and a reason, for the Christmas issue.

Let's Go Neighboring

Leah Neustadt

THIS IS A country story, about a Christmas away back in 1876.

Uncle Barney was a just and kind man in his ideas of right and wrong. His nearest neighbor was Ed Newton, a good farmer, who had a severe struggle to get along.

Ed Newton watered his milk and was caught at it. You would have to be country bred to know the enormity of the offense. It was on a par with horse stealing, and men have been hanged for that. But we are not all built with stiff backs and incorruptible morals. Ed Newton fell, and was detected. It required money and influence and the pleading and tears of a distracted wife to keep him out of jail. After that he was kept in fierce isolation by his neighbors.

There is no more cruel sentence than to be ignored. When Ed and his family were left alone, Newton became a silent, aged, down-cast man who went into the next town to buy his groceries, and have his horses shod. He walked with his head down.

That nearly killed Mary, Ed's wife. She was never again seen at church or at any meetings. You never saw lights in the Newton house at night and Mrs. Newton nursed one of her girls back from the portals of death without even calling the doctor.

The Christmas of 1876 was a stem-winder, with the wind blowing great guns, and the snow drifting until the fences were lost, and the roads almost obliterated. It was bitter cold and the children were sent home from the little red school house. Four inches of ice on the pond had to be chopped through, so the cattle could drink. In the morning came the Christmas calm, the sun shone, and God Almighty showed what a wonderful picture He could make when He set His mind to it.

Simple gifts had been hung in front of the fire-place and there were raisin clusters, stick candy, peanuts, and a great deal of the greatest gift of all, human love in a happy home. The chores had been done, and Uncle Barney sat by the fire toasting his shins, and thinking. His face looked like a graven image, if I know what a graven image is. He kicked off his slippers and reached for his boots.

"Miriam," he said in his rich voice, "you and me and all the children are going visiting. Ed Newton has lived in hell long enough. Even God Almighty don't aim to condemn a man for one slip. Get the dinner fixings together for we are going to eat our Christmas dinner where we ain't invited."

He chuckled and then said, "Maybe I don't look much like a good Samaritan, but I'm going over to try to move a load off a man's heart."

"You are a good and blessed man," came the voice from the kitchen. The children helped to hitch the horse to the big bob-sled with straw in the box and blankets and robes. And the turkey and mince pies were loaded in the clothes basket. Uncle Barney stamped back into the barn and came out with 2 strings of sleigh bells, which he hung on the necks of the snorting horses. Away they all went, down the road, snow flying, crisp air making their cheeks tingle, bells making music, and they swung in the Newton driveway and through a great draft and were at the side door, almost before you could say "Jack Robinson!"

The two women cried out, "Miriam!" and "Mary!" and threw their arms about each other, crying.

Then Uncle Barney said, "We've come neighboring, Ed, just as we used to do, and we want this to be a Merry Christmas for all of us, who need each other and who like each other."

Ed Newton went over to the settee and held his head in his hands, then he got up and kissed his wife and Aunt Miriam and all the girls. And the children got together and played and showed each other's gifts. All the strangeness disappeared.

The women folks then went into the house and started on dinner, while the men folks went out to the barn to look at the stock. The children played in the snow and had a bully time. At last, Mrs.

Newton rang the big farm bell on the kitchen roof and they all gathered for Christmas dinner.

Ed Newton said the blessing and choked up so badly that he could hardly get through with it, and his wife laid her worn hand on his while he was praying. Yes, siree, that was some dinner, with two helpings of everything and cider and apples, and nuts in the parlor afterwards.

Well the best of things come to an end. Uncle Barney and his family had to go home for their chores. But visits were promised and all the old troubles were buried deep under the snow, and out of sight. There was more kissing and as Uncle Barney turned back for another handshake, he said, "May God bless this house and all who are in it."

Back in his home, he raked the fire into a blaze and went out and cared for all the animals about the place as becomes a good farmer.

As Uncle Barney started for bed, Aunt Miriam said, "Barney, you are a good man, a blessed good man. God cannot forget what you have done this day."

A Fragile Moment

E.L. Huffine

THE TELEGRAM was waiting for me: "Imperative training completed soon as possible. No Christmas leaves authorized."

Then, just before my commanding officer's name, there were the ironic words, "Merry Christmas."

So that was that. There would be no chance to get home, no chance even to try for a little holiday feeling in this fearful year. I was an Army pilot on assignment for special training in celestial navigation at Chicago's Adler Planetarium. This was December, 1941. Our nation had been in World War II for only a few weeks.

Ours was a gloomy bunch that gathered for study in the Planetarium's viewing arena that Christmas Eve. Our teacher realized when she came out to speak that we were not the most receptive of classes.

"Gentlemen," she said, "this is going to be an unusual session. Our engineers have been working since the early hours of this morning in an effort to produce what you are about to see. They want you to accept it as their Christmas gift to you."

Slowly the lights lowered and overhead the stars appeared in view, brighter and brighter, until we were deep in a panorama of dazzling beauty.

"Here are the heavens," the teacher said, her voice soft, her tone reverent. "Here are the heavens just as they were that night when Christ Jesus was born."

Except for a howling wind outside, not a sound could be heard. We stared with the kind of wonder that the shepherds must have known two thousand years earlier. In the midst of war I had a vision of peace and of hope for a sick world that left me breathless.

When the lights came up again, we left the auditorium in silence. Our gloom was lost as such things are always lost when we let the fact of His birth take over.

The Love That Lives

Every child on earth is holy,
Every crib is a manger lowly,
Every home is a stable dim,
Every kind word is a hymn,
Every star is God's own gem,
And every town is Bethlehem,
For Christ is born and born again,
When His love lives in hearts of men.

W.D. Dorrity

IX
CHRISTMAS
A Time for Love

Christmas is a time for love,

A time for inhibitions to shed,

A time for showing that we care,

A time for words too long unsaid.

Three Symbols of Christmas

Billy Graham

THERE ARE three symbols which mean Christmas—the real meaning of Christmas.

The first is a *cradle*. There, in Bethlehem, were cradled the hopes and dreams of a dying world. Those chubby little hands that clasped the straw in His manger crib were soon to open blind eyes, unstop deaf ears and still the troubled seas. That cooing voice was soon to teach men of the Way and to raise the dead. Those tiny feet were to take Him to the sick and needy and were to be pierced on Calvary's cross.

That manger crib in remote Bethlehem became the link that bound a lost world to a loving God.

The *cross*. There were both light and shadow on that first Christmas. There was joy with overtones of sadness, for Jesus was born to die. Jesus, approaching the cross, said, *To this end was I born, and for this cause came I into the world*. To Christians the joy of Christmas is not limited to His birth. It was His death and resurrection that gave meaning to His birth.

178

It is in the cross that the world can find a solution to its pressing problems.

The *crown*. Jesus was crowned with a crown of thorns and enthroned on a cruel cross, yet His assassins did something, perhaps unwittingly. They placed a superscription over His cross in Greek, Latin and Hebrew: "This is the King."

Yes, Christ is King of kings and Lord of lords, and He is coming back someday. He will come not as a babe in Bethlehem's manger. The next time He comes it will be in a blaze of glory and He will be crowned Lord of all.

Cradle—cross—crown. Let them speak to you. Let the power of Him who came to us at Christmas grip *you*, and He will surely change your life.

What the Star Tells Us

Fulton J. Sheen

WHY DID the Christ Child come?" is a question we often hear at Christmas time. Let us imagine that the star over the crib is five-pointed, and that this light from heaven issued forth five rays which were the reasons for the Christ Child coming to earth.

The first ray was that now God was tabernacled among men. Proud man, who distorted his nature by defying himself, was given the lesson of Divinity appearing as the servant of man, coming not to be ministered unto, but to minister.

The second ray was His sacrifice. He did not come to live; He came to die. The sin of mankind merited death, for the wages of sin is death. He would take on the sins of man as if they were His own; their blasphemies, as if His lips had spoken them; their thefts, as if His own hands committed them. He became the Good Shepherd Who lays down His life for His sheep.

The third ray was His mercy and compassion and sympathy. He knew human hearts because He made them. Hence His deep love for sinners whom society condemned, and His condemnation of those who sinned and denied they were sinners, or else who sinned but had not yet been found out. Humanity was wounded, but not all men admitted their wounds. But to all who saw their guilt and came to Him, He was the Physician Who restored their souls to union with Himself.

The fourth ray was the establishment of a kingdom which would be a prolongation of His own body. . . . As He taught, as He governed, as He sanctified through other human natures who would be His apostles and their successors, He would continue to teach, to govern and to sanctify.

The fifth ray was His promise to live within us. If He remained on earth, He would have been only an example to be copied; we could have got no closer to Him than an embrace or a word. But if He went back to Heaven and sent His Spirit, then He would be an example to be lived. Those who possess that Spirit of Christ today, manifesting His humility, compassion, sacrifice and love as He did, are really celebrating the Christmas.

The Gift of Double Joy

Linda Leighton

IT HAPPENED in 1958. That fall, when my husband, Joe, and I were making out our Christmas shopping list, we suddenly realized that our giving had become almost routine. We wanted to remember our friends at Christmas but we had little enthusiasm for the usual exchange of ties and trinkets.

Then at our church (St. James Presbyterian) we heard a Korean missionary tell of the thousands of destitute refugee children. An idea was born. All our presents would go to these children.

Here, we felt, was a way to really "put Christ back into Christmas."

A missionary in Korea provided us with names, ages, sex and measurements of 35 children. We sent gifts, each bearing the name of one of our friends as the giver. A greeting card from us to our friends announced the gift and the address of the child to whom it had gone.

Many of our friends began correspondence with these youngsters. The idea has spread to others in our church and outside as well.

Every Christmas is now an exciting experience as we find new names of children and new givers. It is surprising—or is it—that this kind of double giving doubles the joy.

X

CHRISTMAS

A Time for Remembering

Christmas is a time to remember

Timeless stories from days of yore,

A time to ponder what's ahead,

A time to open another door.

The Man Who Missed Christmas

J. Edgar Parks[2*]

ON CHRISTMAS Eve, as usual, George Mason was the last to leave the office. He stood for a moment at the window, watching the hurrying crowds below, the strings of colored Christmas lights, the fat Santa Clauses on the street corners. He was a slender man in his late thirties, this George Mason, not conspicuously successful or brilliant, but a good executive—he ran his office efficiently and well.

Abruptly he turned and walked over to a massive safe set into the far wall. He spun the dials, swung the heavy door open. A light went on, revealing a vault of polished steel as large as a small room. George Mason carefully propped a chair against the open door of the safe and stepped inside.

He took three steps forward, tilting his head so that he could see the square of white cardboard taped just above the topmost row of strongboxes. On the card a few words were written. George Mason stared at those words, remembering. . . .

Exactly one year ago he had entered this selfsame vault. He had planned a rather expensive, if solitary, evening; had decided he might

2* Adapted by Arthur Gordon

need a little additional cash. He had not bothered to prop the door; ordinarily friction held the balanced mass of metal in place. But only that morning the people who serviced the safe had cleaned and oiled it. And then, behind George Mason's back, slowly, noiselessly, the ponderous door swung shut. There was a click of springlocks. The automatic light went out, and he was trapped—entombed in the sudden and terrifying dark.

Instantly, panic seized him. He hurled himself at the unyielding door. He gave a hoarse cry; the sound was like an explosion in that confined place. In the silence that followed, he heard the frantic thudding of his heart. Through his mind flashed all the stories he had heard of men found suffocated in timevaults. No timeclock controlled this mechanism; the safe would remain locked until it was opened from the outside. Tomorrow morning.

Then the sickening realization struck him. No one would come tomorrow morning—tomorrow was Christmas Day.

Once more he flung himself at the door, shouting wildly, beating with his hands until he sank on his knees exhausted. Silence again; high-pitched, singing silence that seemed deafening.

George Mason was no smoker; he did not carry matches. Except for the tiny luminous dial of his watch, the darkness was absolute. The blackness almost had texture: it was tangible, stifling. The time now was 6:15. More than 36 hours would pass before anyone entered the office. Thirty-six hours in a steel box

three feet wide, eight feet long, seven feet high. Would the oxy-
gen last, or would . . .

Like a flash of lightning a memory came to him, dim with the
passage of time. What had they told him when they installed the
safe? Something about a safety measure for just such a crisis as this.

Breathing heavily, he felt his way around the floor. The palms
of his hands were sweating. But in the far righthand corner, just above
the floor, he found it: a small, circular opening some two inches in
diameter. He thrust his finger into it and felt, faint but mistakable,
a cool current of air.

The tension release was so sudden that he burst into tears. But
at last he sat up. Surely he would not have to stay trapped for the
full 36 hours. Somebody would miss him, would make inquiries,
would come to release him. . . .

But who? He was unmarried and lived alone. The maid who
cleaned his apartment was just a servant; he had always treated her
as such. He had been invited to spend Christmas Eve with his brother's
family, but children got on his nerves, and expected presents.

A friend had asked him to go to a home for elderly people on
Christmas Day and play the piano—George Mason was a good musi-
cian. But he had made some excuse or other; he had intended to sit
at home with a good cigar, listening to some new recordings he was
giving himself for Christmas.

George Mason dug his nails into the palms of his hands until the pain balanced the misery in his mind. He had thrown away his chances. Nobody would come and let him out. Nobody, nobody . . .

Marked by the luminous hands of the watch, the leaden-footed seconds ticked away. He slept a little, but not much. He felt no hunger, but he was tormented by thirst. Miserably the whole of Christmas Day went by, and the succeeding night. . . .

On the morning after Christmas the head clerk came into the office at the usual time. He opened the safe but did not bother to swing the heavy door wide. Then he went on into his private office.

No one saw George Mason stagger out into the corridor, run to the water cooler, and drink great gulps of water. No one paid any attention to him as he descended to the street and took a taxi home.

There he shaved, changed his wrinkled clothes, ate some break-fast and returned to his office, where his employees greeted him pleas-antly but casually.

On his way to lunch that day he met several acquaintances, but not a single one had noticed his Christmas absence. He even met his own brother, who was a member of the same luncheon club, but his brother failed to ask if he had enjoyed Christmas.

Grimly, inexorably, the truth closed in on George Mason. He had vanished from human society during the great festival of broth-erhood and fellowship, and no one had missed him at all.

Reluctantly, almost with a sense of dread, George Mason began to think about the true meaning of Christmas. Was it possible that he had been blind all these years, blind with selfishness, with indifference, with pride? Wasn't Christmas the time when men went out of their way to share with one another the joy of Christ's birth? Wasn't giving, after all, the essence of Christmas because it marked the time God gave His own Son to the world?

All through the year that followed, with little hesitant deeds of kindness, with small, unnoticed acts of unselfishness, George Mason tried to prepare himself. . . .

Now, once more, it was Christmas Eve.

Slowly he backed out of the safe, closed it. He touched its grim steel face lightly, almost affectionately, as if it were an old friend. He picked up his hat and coat, and certain bundles. Then he left the office, descended to the busy street.

There he goes now in his black overcoat and hat, the same George Mason as a year ago. Or is it? He walks a few blocks, then flags a taxi, anxious not to be late. His nephews are expecting him to help them trim the tree. Afterwards, he is taking his brother and his sister-in-law to a Christmas play. Why is he so inexpressibly happy? Why does those jostling against others, laden as he is with bundles, exhilarate and delight him?

Perhaps the card has something to do with it, the card he taped inside his office safe last New Year's Day. On the card is written, in George Mason's own hand: *To love people, to be indispensable some-where, that is the purpose of life. That is the secret of happiness.*

The Miraculous Staircase

Arthur Gordon

ON THAT cool December morning in 1878, sunlight lay like an amber rug across the dusty streets and adobe houses of Santa Fe. It glinted on the bright tile roof of the almost completed Chapel of Our Lady of Light and on the nearby windows of the convent school run by the Sisters of Loretto. Inside the convent, the Mother Superior looked up from her packing as a tap came on her door.

"It's *another* carpenter, Reverend Mother," said Sister Francis Louise, her round face apologetic. "I told him that you're leaving right away, that you haven't time to see him, but he says. . . ."

"I know what he says," Mother Magdalene said, going on resolutely with her packing. "That he's heard about our problem with the new chapel. That he's the best carpenter in all of New Mexico. That he can build us a staircase to the choir loft despite the fact that the brilliant architect in Paris who drew the plans failed to leave any space for one. And despite the fact that five master carpenters have already tried and failed. You're quite right, Sister; I don't have time to listen to that story again."

"But he seems such a nice man," said Sister Francis Louise wistfully, "and he's out there with his burro, and . . ."

"I'm sure," said Mother Magdalene with a smile, "that he's a charming man, and that his burro is a charming donkey. But there's sickness down at the Santo Domingo pueblo, and it may be cholera. Sister Mary Helen and I are the only ones here who've had cholera. So we have to go. And you have to stay and run the school. And that's that!" Then she called, "Manuela!"

A young Indian girl of 12 or 13, black-haired and smiling, came in quietly on moccasined feet. She was a mute. She could hear and understand, but the Sisters had been unable to teach her to speak. The Mother Superior spoke to her gently: "Take my things down to the wagon, child. I'll be right there." And to Sister Francis Louise: "You'd better tell your carpenter friend to come back in two or three weeks. I'll see him then."

"Two or three weeks! Surely you'll be home for Christmas?"

"If it's the Lord's will, Sister. I hope so."

In the street, beyond the waiting wagon, Mother Magdalene could see the carpenter, a bearded man, strongly built and taller than most Mexicans, with dark eyes and a smiling, wind-burned face. Beside him, laden with tools and scraps of lumber, a small gray burro stood patiently. Manuela was stroking its nose, glancing shyly at its owner. "You'd better explain," said the Mother Superior, "that the child can hear him, but she can't speak."

193

Goodbyes were quick—the best kind when you leave a place you love. Southwest, then, along the dusty trail, the mountains purple with shadow, the Rio Grande a ribbon of green far off to the right. The pace was slow, but Mother Magdalene and Sister Mary Helen amused themselves by singing songs and telling Christmas stories as the sun marched up and down the sky. And their leathery driver listened and nodded.

Two days of this brought them to Santo Domingo Pueblo, where the sickness was not cholera after all, but measles, almost as deadly in an Indian village. And so they stayed, helping the harassed Father Sebastian, visiting the dark adobe hovels where feverish brown children tossed and fierce Indian dogs showed their teeth.

At night they were boneweary, but sometimes Mother Magdalene found time to talk to Father Sebastian about her plans for the dedication of the new chapel. It was to be in April; the Archbishop himself would be there. And it might have been dedicated sooner, were it not for this incredible business of a choir loft with no means of access—unless it were a ladder.

"I told the Bishop," said Mother Magdalene, "that it would be a mistake to have the plans drawn in Paris. If something went wrong, what could we do? But he wanted our chapel in Santa Fe patterned after the Sainte Chapelle in Paris, and who am I to argue with Bishop Lamy? So the talented Monsieur Mouly designs a beautiful choir loft high up under the rose window, and no way to get up to it."

"Perhaps," sighed Father Sebastian, "he had in mind a heavenly choir. The kind with wings."

"It's not funny," said Mother Magdalene a bit sharply. "I've prayed and prayed, but apparently there's no solution at all. There just isn't room on the chapel floor for the supports such a staircase needs."

The days passed, and with each passing day Christmas drew closer. Twice, horsemen on their way from Santa Fe to Albuquerque brought letters from Sister Francis Louise. All was well at the convent, but Mother Magdalene frowned over certain paragraphs. "The children are getting ready for Christmas," Sister Francis Louise wrote in her first letter. "Our little Manuela and the carpenter have become great friends. It's amazing how much he seems to know about us all. . . ."

And what, thought Mother Magdalene, is the carpenter still doing there?

The second letter also mentioned the carpenter. "Early every morning he comes with another load of lumber, and every night he goes away. When we ask him by what authority he does these things, he smiles and says nothing. We have tried to pay him for his work, but he will accept no pay. . . ."

Work? What work? Mother Magdalene wrinkled up her nose in exasperation. Had that softhearted Sister Francis Louise given the man permission to putter around in the new chapel? With firm and disapproving hand the Mother Superior wrote a note ordering an end to all such unauthorized activities. She gave it to an Indian pottery-maker on his way to Santa Fe.

But that night the first snow fell, so thick and heavy that the Indian turned back. Next day at noon the sun shone again on a world glittering with diamonds. But Mother Magdalene knew that another snowfall might make it impossible for her to be home for Christmas. By now the sickness at Santo Domingo was subsiding. And so that afternoon they began the long ride back.

The snow did come again, making their slow progress even slower. It was late on Christmas Eve, close to midnight, when the tired horses plodded up to the convent door. But lamps still burned. Manuela flew down the steps, Sister Francis Louise close behind her. And chilled and weary though she was, Mother Magdalene sensed instantly an excitement, an electricity in the air that she could not understand.

Nor did she understand it when they led her, still in her heavy wraps, down the corridor, into the new, as-yet-unused chapel where a few candles burned. "Look Reverend Mother," breathed Sister Francis Louise. "Look!"

Like a curl of smoke the staircase rose before them, as insubstantial as a dream. Its base was on the chapel floor; its top rested against the choir loft. Nothing else supported it; it seemed to float on air. There were no banisters. Two complete spirals it made, the polished wood gleaming softly in the candlelight. "Thirty-three steps," whispered Sister Francis Louise. "One for each year in the life of Our Lord."

Mother Magdalene moved forward like a woman in a trance. She put her foot on the first step, then the second, then the third. There was not a tremor. She looked down, bewildered, at Manuela's ecstatic, upturned face. "But it's impossible! There wasn't time!"

"He finished yesterday," the Sister said. "He didn't come today. No one has seen him anywhere in Santa Fe. He's gone."

"But *who* was he? Don't you even know his *name*?"

The Sister shook her head, but now Manuela pushed forward, nodding emphatically. Her mouth opened; she took a deep, shuddering breath; she made a sound that was like a gasp in the stillness. The nuns stared at her, transfixed. She tried again. This time it was a syllable, followed by another. "Jo-sé." She clutched the Mother Superior's arm and repeated the first word she had ever spoken. "José!"

Sister Francis Louise crossed herself. Mother Magdalene felt her heart contract. José—the Spanish word for Joseph. Joseph the Carpenter. Joseph the Master Woodworker of . . .

"José!" Manuela's dark eyes were full of tears. "José!"

Silence, then, in the shadowy chapel. No one moved. Far away across the snow-silvered town Mother Magdalene heard a bell tolling midnight. She came down the stairs and took Manuela's hand. She felt uplifted by a great surge of wonder and gratitude and compassion and love. And she knew what it was. It was the spirit of Christmas. And it was upon them all.

Author's Note: The wonderful thing about legends is the way they grow. Through the years they can be told and retold and embroidered a bit more each time. This, indeed, is such a retelling. But all good legends contain a grain of truth, and in this case the irrefutable fact at the heart of the legend is the inexplicable staircase itself.

You may see it yourself in Santa Fe today. It stands just as it stood when the chapel was dedicated except for the banister, which was added later. Tourists stare and marvel. Architects shake their heads and murmur, "Impossible." No one knows the identity of the designer-builder. All the Sisters know is that the problem existed, a stranger came, solved it and left.

The 33 steps make two complete turns without central support. There are no nails in the staircase; only wooden pegs. The curved stringers are put together with exquisite precision; the wood is spliced in seven places on the inside and nine on the outside. The wood is said to be a hard-fir variety, nonexistent in New Mexico. School records show that no payment for the staircase was ever made.

Who is real and who is imaginary in this version of the story? Mother Mary Magdalene was indeed the first Mother Superior; she came to Santa Fe by riverboat and covered wagon in 1852. Bishop J. B. Lamy was indeed her Bishop. And Monsieur Projectus Mouly of Paris was indeed the absentminded architect.

Sister Francis Louise? Well, there must have been someone like her. And Manuela, the Indian girl, came out of nowhere to help with the embroidery.

The carpenter himself? Ah, who can say?

The Runaway Boy

Chase Walker

THERE IS something about a holiday that turns normally silent people—total strangers—into secret-confiding friends.

Such was the case one Christmas Eve not long ago aboard a speeding Midwestern train. The electric spirit of the season seemed to fill each car. In one seat, a little girl, sporting a big yellow bow in her hair, asked anxiously, "How much longer to Grandma's?"

A few seats away, a sailor proudly held out a wallet-sized photograph of his sweetheart, showing it to the others around him.

Everyone seemed to be talking and laughing. Everyone except one young man and his seat companion, a kindly looking gentleman with gray-white hair. The man had vainly attempted to start a conversation, but the boy was preoccupied. He never looked away from the window.

Finally, the man gave up and went back to reading his book—until he realized the young man was crying, a muffled, quiet crying, but unmistakably crying.

"Need a handkerchief?" the man asked.

"Yes, sir," answered the boy. "Thank you."

There was a moment's silence.

"Is there anything I can do, Son?"

"No, I'm afraid not. It's too late. . . ." The boy put the handkerchief to his face again.

Placing his hand on the boy's shoulder, the man consoled him, "Sometimes we only think it's too late. Why don't you tell me the problem. Let me decide."

"Well . . ." the boy hesitated, then began:

"It was four months ago . . . well, almost four months. You see, I ran away from home. I just couldn't take it anymore . . . my school work was horrible . . . and I was sick to death of doing chores morning and night. Well, I told Dad and we had a terrible argument. That night I packed some clothes and headed for the city. I had a little money saved and figured I could get a job. In less than a week I realized that I had made a mistake. I was tempted to tell Mom and Dad that I wanted to come home when I wrote them not to worry, but I was too embarrassed. Many nights I slept in the streets, hungry more often than not."

The boy blew his nose and dabbed at his eyes again. "Finally, last week I broke down and wrote Dad that I wanted to come home, though I knew he might not want me back. I told him I'd be on this train, and that if I was welcome he should tie a red cloth on the big elm at the back of the farm. The train runs right past our farm and that old tree drapes over the fence."

"Well, I think you'll be welcome, Son," the man assured him. Picking up the book which had lain in his lap, the old man leafed through it. "You probably think your story is unique, but in this book, this Bible, there is a story much like yours. It's the story of the Prodigal Son. Do you know it?"

The boy shook his head no.

"Then I want to read it to you." And the old man read that familiar story. When he had finished, the boy's face wore a smile.

"I believe most fathers are filled with the same forgiving spirit as in this story," the man said, "and I believe your father will be more than willing to have you back."

The boy suddenly sat upright. "We're almost there," he said. "Our place is right after the next bend. Oh, I'm afraid to look."

"Then I'll look for you," volunteered the man.

The telephone poles raced by. For a moment the man's faith wavered. What if there were no signal in the elm tree?

Just then the train swung around the bend and up ahead he saw the huge elm dancing in the wind, its branches bare against the steel-gray sky and snowy fields. Bare—except for dozens of red banners that flapped from every conceivable limb. They shouted the news to a runaway boy that all was forgiven at Christmas.

A New Year's Prayer

Dear Lord, please give me . . .
A few friends who understand me and yet remain my friends
A work to do which has real value, without which the world would
feel the poorer . . .
A mind unafraid to travel, even though the trail be not blazed
An understanding heart . . .
A sense of humor.
Time for quiet, silent meditation.
A feeling of the presence of God.
And the patience to wait for the coming of these things, with the
wisdom to know them when they come.

W.R. Hunt

The Greatest Story Ever Told

Saint Luke

AND JOSEPH also went up from Galilee, out of the city of Nazareth, into Judaea, unto the city of David, which is called Bethlehem . . . to be taxed with Mary his espoused wife, being great with child.

And so it was, that, while they were there, the days were accomplished that she should be delivered.

And she brought forth her firstborn Son, and wrapped Him in swaddling clothes, and laid Him in a manger; because there was no room for them in the inn.

And there were in the same country shepherds abiding in the field, keeping watch over their flock by night.

And, lo, the angel of the Lord came upon them, and the glory of the Lord shone round about them: and they were sore afraid.

And the angel said unto them, Fear not: for, behold, I bring you good tidings of great joy, which shall be to all people.

For unto you is born this day in the city of David a Saviour, which is Christ the Lord.

And this shall be a sign unto you; Ye shall find the Babe wrapped in swaddling clothes, lying in a manger.

And suddenly there was with the angel a multitude of the heavenly host praising God, and saying, Glory to God in the highest, and on earth peace, good will toward men.